THE DEVILS SMELLED NICE
THE COMPLETE ADVENTURES
OF THE GADGET MAN, VOLUME 2

THE DEVILS SMELLED NICE

THE COMPLETE ADVENTURES OF THE GADGET MAN, VOLUME 2

LESTER DENT

PRIMARY ILLUSTRATOR: ALBERT MICALE

ALTUS PRESS

2023

TABLE OF CONTENTS

INTRODUCTION

BOTH THE SHADOW'S creator Walter B. Gibson and his editor, John L. Nanovic, claimed to have conceived the idea that ultimately led to the creation of *Crime Busters,* and indirectly Lester Dent's Gadget Man series.

Street and Smith was searching for a new type of magazine, one that would showcase a strong hero, like *The Shadow* or *Doc Savage*. But in the Roosevelt Recession of 1937-38, new titles were a risky venture.

Gibson's idea was a "seed" magazine featuring three new heroes by top S&S writers. If any one grew popular, his thinking went, that character could be spun off into his own title and replaced by a new candidate.

> "I was talking to [S&S Business Manager Henry] Ralston about more character magazines," Gibson explained. "And I was thinking myself of a magician detective, though I didn't know how it would go. He said, 'Well, it's costly to start a character magazine, and if it flops....' So I suggested that they put out one with three characters in it. And then whichever one went well, that would be it. They went ahead, but they put in five or six characters. Everyone else used his own name, even Lester Dent with his Bufa stories, but they asked me if I would put on the 'Maxwell Grant' because then

they would advertise it in the Shadow magazine—'Get the stories by Maxwell Grant'—so it was really a favor to them on my part."

Nanovic recalled it this way:

"That was mostly my idea," he said. "And I don't want to brag about it because it didn't do too well. It just got along. Here we had a stable of famous writers. Gibson. Robeson. All of them were selling pretty well. So I said, 'The guys who like these fellas should like them in other magazines.' So we made up *Crime Busters*. These were all lead house names. We had like ten in every issue."

Henry W. Ralston and editor Nanovic ultimately decided to run more, shorter tales in what they dubbed *Crime Busters*. Gibson already had a character in mind, a traveling magician-sleuth named Norgil, which he wrote under the house name of Maxwell Grant. Ted Tinsley was contacted and created Carrie Cashin, a strong female detective. He did this under his own name.

No doubt Lester Dent was high on the list of writers S&S recruited for *Crime Busters*. His Doc Savage novels had been popular for four years. No doubt also, S&S attempted to prevail upon Dent to write the new series under the Kenneth Robeson house name. There is no doubt Dent resisted strenuously. He hated the Robeson byline, was initially surprised when the name was attached to his early Doc novels. Dent stood firm. He would contribute to the new magazine as Dent, or not at all.

Dent was a formula writer. He also loved gadgets. And by 1937 had developed a kind of screwball humor approach to Doc Savage.

From the little we know about it, a lot can be inferred about the genesis of Click Rush, the Gadget Man.

Sometime in 1936 but no later than June, 1937, Lester Dent rolled a carbon-paper sandwich into his Remington typewriter and rattled off the following:

TALKING DOG

The block of stone was about five feet long, two feet wide, and a foot thick. It was granite. It probably weighed over a ton.

It fell fifteen stories and missed John Magic by the length of an arm.

There was a crash. A hole burst open in the sidewalk, dust puffed and pieces of rock flew about, and across the street a man let out a yell. Or bleat.

Whether Dent changed his mind in mid-stride, or kept writing is unknown. Only this variant first page survived among his manuscripts.

During Dent's 1936 sabbatical from writing Doc Savage, he cracked several prestigious markets, including *Argosy* and *Black Mask*. He tried but failed to break into *Detective Fiction Weekly*. There is an excellent chance that the unpublished "Talking Dog" was a *DFW* reject that Dent dusted off when the *Crime Busters* opportunity arose.

It's possible Dent took the first adventure featuring John Magic into John Nanovic's office and got into a disagreement over the appropriate byline.

Whatever the case, in mid-June of 1937, Dent submitted "Talking Toad," the first adventure of Clickell Rush, the Gadget Man.

If the subject of the Kenneth Robeson byline came up that this point, Dent was prepared to hold his ground with Nanovic. Back in 1930, he had penned a novel featuring a San Francisco reporter named Click Rush. "The Thirteen Million Dollar Robbery" appeared in S&S's *The Popular*

Magazine. A sequel, "The Phantom Lagoon," was rejected and the manuscript since been lost. Since it was his character, Click Rush's new adventures would carry Dent's name. Lester had not forgotten his surprise and disappointment when his first Doc Savage novel was published under the short-lived house name of Kenneth Roberts. No one had told him in advance.

Whether or not this Click Rush is precisely the same character is open to question. There's not enough description and background in the 1930 novel to definitely say one way or another. The chief difference was that the Click Rush who battled through "The Thirteen Million Dollar Robbery" and its unpublished sequel was a true pulp hero.

Nanovic remembered Dent telling him he'd used the character before.

> "He did do those stories for somebody else before—I think," Nanovic related. "See, he wrote a lot of stuff. I think this was a character he wrote before and picked it up and put in here. He didn't do many of them, one or two."

Whatever the case, Dent stuck to his guns——and his true byline.

"Talking Toad" lead off the first issue of the new title, November 1937. (An excerpt had run in the last issue of *Best Detective,* the magazine *Crime Busters* replaced.) Included in Volume 1 Number 1 was coupon to entice reader reaction to the new set of characters.

Response was enthusiastic. Gadget Man was consistently one of the top reader favorites, with Norgil the magician and Carrie Cashin following a close second. Ironically, Norgil came in third. With these results in, Nanovic ordered his writers to expand the lengths of their stories, and this oddball trio became the spine of *Crime Busters*.

The premise of the Gadget Man seems to be a screwball variation on the original screwball detective, Nick Charles, hero of Dashiell Hammett's popular novel, *The Thin Man*. Rex Stout's Nero Wolfe novels—which Dent also read and admired—might have also supplied some inspiration. The mysterious Bufa was Wolfe, with poor Click Rush an unwilling Archie Goodwin.

The reincarnated Rush was a reluctant hero.

Gadget detectives had been a Dent staple since his 1932 *Detective-Dragnet* series about scientific criminologist Lynn Lash. A year later, there was Lee Nace, known as the "Blond Adder," in *Ten Detective Aces*. And in 1934, Foster Fade, the Crime Spectacularist, ran briefly in Dell's *All-Detective Magazine*.

Where did Dent get this idea? Well, his mother was a great gadgeteer, capable of building crystal radios and electrical chicken-coop warmers. Dent's lifelong love of tools and gadgets stemmed from her mechanically-inclined influence.

In literary terms, inspiration can be split between Arthur B. Reeve's pioneering scientific sleuth, Craig Kennedy, and Erle Stanley Gardner whose pulp heroes often relied on simple tricks like teargas fountain pens and the like.

Headquartered in the Imperial Apartments in Manhattan's Central Park West—where Dent lived on and off during the 1930s—Click Rush roamed around the country solving crimes with gadgets and electrical devices right out of Doc Savage.

Rush had no interest in solving crimes. He was an inventor. His life goal was to sell his crook-catching gadgets to police agencies, and thereby grow prosperous. Enter Bufa.

One day Rush discovers large papier-mâché toad in his room. It comes with instructions to plug it in and insert a light bulb into its gaping mouth. Turns out it's a radio receiver that operates through city electrical wiring. The toad starts speaking:

> *"Hello,"* the toad said. *"You are, I presume, Mr. Rush?"*
>
> Rush frowned and leaned close to the toad. "Of all the damned fool things, this mess takes the prize. Someone is crazy. Nuts."
>
> *"I am Bufa,"* said the toad, *"of the species* Bufonidæ, *which feeds upon snails, slugs, insects, and such undesirable things."*
>
> *"Bufonidæ,"* Rush growled, "is the scientific name for the toad species. What has that got to do with this insane mess?"
>
> *"I am Bufa. I feed on snails, slugs, et cetera—of the human variety."*
>
> "Sure," Rush said. "That's all right. I suppose the keepers from whatever bughouse you got out of will find you eventually."
>
> *"You don't have much imagination, do you?"*
>
> "If it takes imagination to make this seem sensible, I'm all out to-day."
>
> There was no way, Rush thought, of locating the other person. Direction-finders would not locate a wired-wireless transmitter.
>
> *"For a long time,"* said the voice, *"I have been thinking of doing something like this."*
>
> "Like what?"
>
> *"Hiring an expert private detective to investigate crimes which I think need solving."*

Half of a ten-thousand dollar bill comes with the toad. Solve the mystery of the stainless steel frogs and the other half will come in the mail. Which a reluctant Rush proceeds to do.

For 18 hilarious episodes, Bufa bribes, bamboozles and otherwise bullies Rush into being his risk-taking legman. For his part, Rush vows to track down and unmask his disembodied tormentor. Their dysfunctional relationship drives the series.

When not succumbing to greed, Rush attempts to ditch the toad in various ways. Always, Bufa locates him. And the shenanigans begin anew. This combination of hard-boiled and screwball storytelling has acquired a modern appellation: "screwboiled."

The man shown examining a dummy head on the illustration heading the second story, "Death in Boxes," bears a striking and suspicious resemblance to Lester Dent himself. I doubt that is a coincidence.

The third adventure is typical. "Funny Faces" begins with the arresting first-line hook: "The man who was collecting noses had no nose himself." And so the faceless Bufa cajoles Rush into investigating a noseless man who had a mania for cutting off snoots of those who did.

The fifth exploit, "Windjam," was set in Dent's Miami dockside haunts where he used to sail. One of the best of this series, it was a salvage job. A story featuring a nautical detective named Cyrus Peace, a rustic corncob-smoking character who operated Admiralty Investigations in Miami, was rejected by *Detective Fiction Weekly*. So Dent converted it into a Click Rush story. Successfully, I might add.

This story was set around Pier No. 4, where Dent's *Black Mask* detective, Oscar Sail, anchored his sloop, and where Dent's *Albatross* spent winters.

"Les was very familiar with that spot," Norma Dent recalled. "Our boat was tied there for two winters. The boat next to ours was a cabin cruiser, owned by the Winchells, (Stewart Sterling) another well-known writer. However, he spent very little time on board his boat. Most of the time he lived in New York."

The *Four Winds* was another vessel anchored nearby. During the 1935 St. Petersburg-to-Havana boat race, Dent crewed on the 47-foot ketch, and spent six long days becalmed in the Gulf of Mexico. No doubt the *Four Winds* was the inspiration for the similarly-named *Fourth Wind* in "Windjam."

The *Albatross* spent her summers at New York's City Island, which is visited in "The Green Birds."

For some reason, toads and frogs keep popping up, as in "The Remarkable Zeke," where the recipient of a package discovers it contains a bullfrog, which he promptly stomps to death. On that thin thread, Dent hangs an entertaining tale.

All went swimmingly for two years. When Dent went to Europe, he took a vacation from Doc Savage. But he kept grinding out Click Rush tales. "The Itching Men" and "The Devils Smelled Nice" were written in Paris, and "Six White Horses," later reprinted in the 1942 *Detective Story Annual,* was inspired by Dent's 1938 European trip. One funny story, "The Monks and the Weasels," was set in LaPlata Missouri, where Dent was born, and where he lived during the final two decades of his life.

But S&S still wanted the Robeson name to appear in *Crime Busters.* So they prevailed on Dent to pen a similar series about an ex-prize fighter and reluctant detective named Ed Stone. Despite the famous byline, readers didn't take to Stone the way they had to Rush. After only seven adventures, Nanovic ordered Dent to concentrate on Click

Rush exclusively. Ed Stone wasn't "clicking," according to Nanovic.

Probably Lester Dent would have continued pounding out Gadget Man novelettes long past the period where *Crime Busters* was retitled *Mystery Magazine* in 1939, but John Nanovic made an unfortunate mistake. He slapped the Kenneth Robeson byline on "The Frightened Yachtsman."

When the story appeared in the September, 1939 Crime Busters, Dent fired off a letter to Nanovic:

> "In reading the current issue of *Crime Busters*, I noticed that the house name, Kenneth Robeson, got on one of the Click Rush yarns. I hope this is an error, because I expended considerable effort in creating the character, and I cannot consent to it appearing under any name other than my own."

Nanovic shot back that the error was actually Dent's. An Ed Stone story had been promised by Dent, but Lester submitted a Click Rush instead. In making up the cover to that issue—covers were always printed before pulp interiors—Nanovic, in his own words, "figured the best way out was to use the name Robeson on it and cross my fingers. We had no comments on it, one way or another. The next Gadget yarn, however, continues under the name of Lester Dent, just as before. That happened to be one of those things."

Nanovic guessed wrong. Very wrong. Readers may not have cared, but Lester Dent did. There was no more correspondence about the matter after that. But the one remaining Gadget Man story on hand ran in *Mystery*, December, 1939. After that there were no more.

One has to assume that Dent was so peeved at the masking of his own byline, he simply stopped writing Gadget Man. There was also a change in buying policy at that point, which would limit a writer's resale options on his own stories, and this new restriction could have played a significant role as well.

If so, this was a terrible tragedy. For this was one of the great screwboiled characters of the pulps. While Dent teased the reader with the true identity of the man behind Bufa, the ubiquitous Talking Toad, he never gave any concrete hints, not even when Rush races to Los Angeles to track down Bufa through the Continental Detective Agency—Dent's nod to his all-time favorite detective writer, Dashiell Hammett, whose nameless Continental Op worked out of their San Francisco office—and comes as close as he ever did to unmasking his tormentor. This took place in "Run, Actor, Run!" and its sequel, "A Man and a Mess."

Ironically, decades after both men had died, Hammett's daughter revealed that her father was a regular reader of *Doc Savage Magazine!* Lester would have been astounded to know that—and no doubt proud.

Alas, we'll never read the Cuban adventure promised at the end of "The Green Birds."

Nor will we ever read a satisfactory conclusion to the series. Readers have speculated that Bufa was Doc Savage or one of is aides, such as electrical wizard Long Tom Roberts. But Dent would never have mixed a series of his own with one owned by S&S, so such speculation is completely out. It's tempting to suggest that this is the philanthropic hero of his *Argosy* serial, Genius Jones. Both Jones and Bufa have a penchant for elliptical speech. Both were created around the same time.

The longest series Lester Dent ever penned, sadly the Gadget Man stories have been neglected for years. And rarely reprinted. Happily, we are changing that lamentable oversight. Additionally, we have gone back to Lester Dent's surviving carbons and restored missing text from every story that suffered editorial cuts for space and other reasons.

In 1940, artist Jack Farr adapted three of Dent's stories for Street & Smith's *Shadow Comics* and *Doc Savage Comics*. The strip was called "The Talking Toad" and Farr probably scripted them himself. Lester Dent never received credit for the feature and I suspect that it stopped after three installments because he complained about it.

As Dent's friend and fellow Street & Smith contributor Frank Gruber once said, "The Gadget Man stories were fantastic and showed a talent for invention that has not been surpassed by any other writer. Harry Stephen Keeler, perhaps, came closest but Lester Dent got as many fantastic tricks in a short story as Harry got in a complete novel."

So who was Bufa? Maybe you reading these fascinating stories can glean a clue from the adventures as they unfold....

—Will Murray

THE HAIRLESS WONDERS

THE GADGET MAN MEETS NOAH—AND
HIS ANCESTORS, IN A COCKEYED
YARN OF THE HAIRLESS WONDERS

CHAPTER I
TROUBLE DRESSED IN MINK

CONCEIVABLY A GREAT many men have had trouble handed to them, and have been surprised—so Clickell Rush was probably no exception. He was surprised.

Likely, also, that men have had difficulties deposited on their hands when least expected, so Click Rush was possibly no exception in that respect, either. He didn't expect it.

The lady wore a mink coat. Ladies in mink coats probably have handed many men some bad shocks.

So Rush should have been alert, up on his toes, and should have lit out running when he saw the lady in the mink coat; but like all the other great goats of history, he didn't perceive this until it was a trifle too late.

The shock the lady in the mink coat handed Rush was disguised as a package, and it was a parcel which looked quite innocent on the outside, being egg-shaped, and as in the case of many an egg, looking harmless enough before it hatched.

"Huh?" Rush said. "Is this for me?"

That was after the lady in the mink coat handed it to him.

By then, she could have handed him almost anything and he would have accepted with enthusiasm, for she was that kind of number. He was taking long looks at her. She was the right length, and had other things that were right.

Her hat was pert and tiny enough that there seemed no reason why it should stay on her coppery-red hair; and her eyes were a deep blue that it would be worth looking into.

Her mouth was provocative, and her chin lines were nice without being firm enough to be discouraging, and while a mink coat is a very enveloping article, the lines of her ankles were promise enough to make any man start wishing she would take the coat off.

Rush said, "Uh—er—hello!"

She said, "You keep it for me."

She meant the package. The parcel was not quite two feet long, half as thick, and not precisely egg shaped—most eggs are a little fatter at one end than the other, and this one wasn't.

Rush was interested in girl, not package.

That is, until something ran around in the package. It ran around fast and made scratching noises, and Rush could tell from that and from the different ways the package felt, that there was something alive inside the thing.

He said, "I—what—*huh?*"

She said, "I'll come back in a few minutes."

The thing stopped running around in the package.

"What's in this?" Rush asked, looking at the package.

"It'll only be a few minutes," the girl said, and started walking backward.

"Hey!" Rush called.

The girl in the mink coat kept on walking backward.

"I'm Clickell Rush," Rush said. "The guy who never saw you before."

"I know who you are." The girl pointed at the parcel. "Do you think I'd give *that* to a perfect stranger?" She went on walking backward.

She walked backward into the elevator, and the elevator doors shut and the indicator over the cage began turning, pausing for a time at the second floor, the third floor and the fourth floor. The hotel had only four floors.

The hotel was the tallest building in Flagstaff, Arizona. **THE THING** began running around in the package again, and Rush looked at the parcel. He had never seen the girl before; he knew of no earthly reason why she should hand him any package, and he did not know what the parcel contained, except that it was something that kept running around.

It didn't make sense.

Rush walked over to the hotel desk. The desk clerk was a round, roly-poly young man with slick blond hair and a neat blond mustache.

"Who am I?" Rush asked.

The blond clerk swallowed, blinked, said, "I—uh—*huh?*"

"Just tell me," Rush said, "who I am."

"If you don't know," the clerk said, "how the hell do you expect me to know?"

Rush said, "I didn't ask you for a damned argument. I asked you a damned question."

"I heard the damned question," the clerk rapped.

"Then give me a damned answer."

"You're on the register as Thomas Gooch," the clerk said. "You wrote the damned name down yourself. How the hell would I know if it's the right one?"

Rush asked, "Do the guests of this hostelry always get damned cussing answers to their questions?"

"Generally they ask sensible questions," the clerk said.

Rush scowled, said, "Way out west, where men are men, huh?" He walked over, carrying the package, and waited for the elevator to come down. The thing in the package ran around some more.

He was down on the register as Thomas Gooch. He had taken a chartered plane up here from El Paso under the name of Thomas Gooch, and nobody on earth, as he knew, was aware that he was Clickell Rush, the fellow who was getting a reputation at solving unusual crimes with gadgets, or that he was in Flagstaff, Arizona, or that he was here for a vacation and nothing else. That didn't make sense, either. He'd told the girl he was Clickell Rush, and she'd said she had known that when she handed him the package with something alive inside.

The elevator came back.

"The redhead," Rush said, "in the mink coat. Where'd she go?"

The elevator operator grinned. "Don't remember her, pard."

Rush handed over a dollar bill.

"That jog your memory any?" he asked.

"She got off at the second floor," the operator said, "after she asked me if there was a back stairs and a back door."

"Back door? And you told her about it—"

"Hell, I told her there was."

RUSH WENT out into the street, carrying the package under his arm, looked around, then walked to the corner and looked around some more. There was nothing interesting, except that the thing in the package moved around some more.

Two cars passed going west, and one passed going east. Two men and two women, dressed like dude ranchers and riding horses, galloped west. A dog lay on the sidewalk with his head in the shade of a telephone pole. The sun was hot.

Rush stood and looked at a store window. Inside the window was an ornate saddle, several bridles, a number of silver-inlaid bridle bits, two coiled lasso ropes, a large flashy sixshooter with holster and cartridge belt, a pair of red mohair chaps and a yellow pair, cowboy boots, big hats, cactus plants, Navajo blankets, and some odds and ends.

Rush studied his own reflection in the window. He saw a man of average height, youngish, with evidence of a remarkable muscular development of the fiddle-string variety visible about his neck and on the backs of his hands.

Rush wore brown cowboy boots, brown pants tucked in the boot tops, a wide, brown cowboy belt with flashy silver adornment, a brown silk shirt, dotted brown handkerchief about the neck, and a brown cowboy hat about twice the size of the one in the window. All this wild west regalia was very new.

"Yippee!" Rush said. "Ride 'em, cowboy!"

He walked back to the hotel with his package and got in the elevator.

"Four," he said.

The elevator started up. The thing in the parcel ran and scratched.

The operator asked, "What you got in there?"

"An esoteric," Rush said.

"Huh?"

"Yep."

The elevator stopped at the fourth floor.

"Male or female?" the operator asked.

"We don't know for sure," Rush explained.

His room was No. 401. He unscrewed the magnifying crystal from his wrist watch, used it to inspect the fingerprint on the chewing gum with which he had sealed the door, decided it was his own fingerprint and that no one had been in the room, and entered.

The cases containing his scientific crook-catching gadgets stood in the center of the room. He scowled at them, wishing the gimmicks inside were not so silly and fantastic, so that he could sell them to some metropolitan police department for a nice piece of change.

Still scowling, he went over and pointed a finger at himself in the mirror.

"You're a better cowboy than you are inventor," he said. "And you never rode a horse in your life."

His mistake had been to invent gadgets so fantastic that only himself could use them to catch crooks with any degree of success.

He took the paper covering off the package.

This revealed an ordinary wire rat trap.

CHAPTER II
ATOM AND NOAH

IT COULD BE a rat. Still, it was a little big for a rat. Also, it had no hair; whereas rats had hair. This thing was just about as hairless as it could be.

Then again, rats didn't have ears like rabbits. But neither did rabbits have long rat-tails.

Rush pointed a finger at the unusual-looking animal in the wire trap and said, *"Ps–s–s!"*

It ran around in the cage like a squirrel.

There was no collar or tag on the animal, no name or identification of any kind on the wire trap, and the paper that had been around the trap was plain brown wrapping paper of a type that could be found in almost any grocery store.

Rush said, "Kitty, kitty, kitty!" and snapped his fingers at the thing in the cage. It didn't do anything. He tried calling it with the noises which are used to summon various kinds of domestic animals and fowls; but nothing happened.

Rush was absent-minded about the calling, as if he did not expect to get results. In the middle of that, there was a rapping on the door.

Rush whipped off his gaudy brown silk cowboy shirt, put on a bulletproof vest which fastened with a zipper, and by that time, the knuckles had made noise on the door again. Rush went to the door.

"Yes," he said.

"Heh, heh," a voice said.

"Eh?"

"I should like to speak to you," the voice said.

"Who is it?"

"Mr. Thomas Gooch," the voice said.

"But I'm Mr. Thomas Gooch," Rush argued.

"Heh, heh," the voice laughed apologetically. "That probably accounts for what I want to talk to you about."

Rush considered, then went over and lighted a cigarette. He never smoked. This cigarette contained, about half way from its end, grains of solidified chemical which, when burned, became a potent tear gas. He hung the cigarette onto his lip and opened the door.

"Heh, heh," the little man outside said cheerfully.

He was a very short and a very wide little man with a long, horselike face and long hands with thick, tapered fingers. His shiny brown shoes were large and long, and his gray Palm Beach suit was neatly creased. His shirt was striped like a stick of candy, and his necktie looked unusually large and gaudy; but that was probably because he was such a short man.

He said, *"Heh, heh,"* again.

Rush said, "I'm glad to meet you, Mr. Thomas Gooch," and extended his hand.

The little man took Rush's hand with both his enthusiastically.

He said, "I'm glad to meet *you* too, Mr. Thomas Gooch."

Still holding to Rush's hand, he walked into the room, looked around, then jumped up off the floor, turned sidewise and kicked Rush in the chest with both feet. Rush lost his cigarette.

It was jiu-jitsu, or tumbling, or high-class wrestling, or something. Anyway, Rush turned over in the air faster than he had ever turned before, and hit the floor harder than he had ever expected to hit a floor.

He got up, and the little man put a foot in his face, pushed, and Rush sat down. Rush got hold of the little man's leg, but not until after the stranger had stepped on the cigarette. The little man did a remarkable contortion, got Rush's ankles with each hand and spread Rush's legs apart. Rush yelped, convinced he was going to split, and hit at the little man. But the little man was gone. He was around behind Rush. He got hold of Rush's head and gave it an osteopathic yank, and it was hours before Rush was convinced his neck was not broken.

The little man stepped back and a big pistol out of his clothing.

My name is really Atom Allen," he said, and added, *"Heh, heh!"*

RUSH SAT on the carpet and wondered if he had a joint or a muscle where there wasn't a hurt. He was full of big agonies and little agonies; he felt as if he had been about half taken apart by a little man who was not half his size.

"Get up," said Atom Allen.

"I don't," Rush said wryly, "think I'm able."

Rush looked at the little man in hopes of seeing something that would explain what the fellow had done to him.

"Atom Allen, eh?" Rush said.

The name did not mean anything—at least, he had never heard it before. He continued to peer at the little man and wonder—he had always considered his own muscular development far above ordinary—how such a midget had bounced him around at will.

Atom Allen said, "Pride hurt, eh?"

"It lost some feathers," Rush admitted.

Atom Allen put his hand which did not hold the gun into a pocket and brought out a bit of metal, which he tossed to Rush. It proved to be a silver half-dollar.

"Give it a gander," he said. "Bite it."

"Eh?"

Atom Allen growled, "Give it the once-over and try to sink your snappers into it. Make sure it's the McCoy."

Rush looked at the half-dollar and bit it.

"The McCoy," he said, and tossed it back.

"Look," Atom Allen said.

The little man took the silver half-dollar in his right hand, closed the hand, and muscles bunched up in the hand like cats arching their backs. Some of the muscle bunches looked as large as lemons. The little man did not grunt or make faces, but his whole arm shook just a little. Then he opened the hand.

The silver half-dollar was folded double.

"Heh, heh," Atom Allen said.

Rush clapped both hands together loudly. "Bravo!" he said. "Now do it to a horseshoe!"

Atom Allen stuck the folded coin in his pocket, put his jaw out.

"I done that for a livin' for years, pal. What's so funny about it?"

Rush thought of the aches and hurts the little man had put in his various joints.

He said, "It's not so funny, on second thought."

Atom Allen came closer. He gave Rush a nudge with the gun snout.

"Where's my wife?" he growled.

Rush said. "Your—*huh?*"

"You wife-stealer!" gritted Atom Allen. "Where is she?"

RUSH FELT behind him for a chair, sank into it, and absently ran his fingers through his hair. His thoughts went round in circles without coming out anywhere.

"Huh?" he said.

Atom Allen gave him a shove. Rush and the chair upset.

"Where's my wife?" Atom Allen snarled.

Rush said, "I don't know where your wife is. All I do know is that you're going to be distributed over this place in small pieces if you keep on the way you're going."

"*Heh!*" said Atom Allen violently. "Up on your feet, brown boy!"

Rush said, "Has your wife got red hair and a mink coat?"

Atom Allen grated, "So you bought her that mink coat!"

"Huh?" Rush said.

"Up on your feet, you *caballero!*"

Rush got up.

"Now," Atom Allen said, "cover your eyes with both hands and just stand there."

Rush covered his eyes with his hands and stood; and the little man removed everything from Rush's pockets, then found the bulletproof vest that Rush wore. He fiddled around trying to get the vest off, did not succeed immediately, and gave it up.

"Rather shoot you in the head, anyway," he said, "—if it comes to shootin'."

Atom Allen walked around the room, looking into the closet, the bath; then he came back to the table and peered at the small, hairless animal in the wire rat trap.

"*Tsk, tsk!*" he clucked sorrowfully. "Poor Noah. Poor, poor, Noah."

Rush said, "Noah?"

The little man peered more closely at the thing in the cage.

"Yep," he said. "This is Noah." He turned around and glared at Rush. "Where's Shem and Ham and Japheth?"

Rush said, "You mean the sons of Noah?"

"Yep."

"Maybe they're still on the ark," Rush said.

The little man scowled.

"This won't be no damn joke when I'm finished with you!" he gritted.

ATOM ALLEN picked up the cage containing the small, strange animal which he had called Noah, and replaced the paper covering which Rush had previously removed from the wire rat trap.

While he was tying the paper in place, Atom Allen said, "I kinda hunched what the wife had in this thing when I saw her walkin' up the street toward this hotel."

"You hunched that she had Noah, eh?" Rush ventured.

"Yep. Noah or one of his sons."

"So you watched her hand Noah over to me?"

"Yep."

"Then you came up to see me and Noah?"

Atom Allen tucked the bundle containing the wire trap and Noah under his left arm, then pointed his gun at Rush.

"Seein' you and Noah is only part of it," he said. "You will now walk out of here with me, get in that elevator, and go where I tell you, acting all the time as if we were good friends."

Rush asked, "Where you taking me?"

"I like to talk in a loud voice."

"But—"

Atom Allen said, "So I'm gonna take you to a place where I can talk in a loud voice if I want to!"

Rush thought of a number of things, not the least of which was that he would probably lay awake nights wondering what this was all bout, if he did not string along with the crazy business until he learned the answers. For the sake of future insomnia, he nodded.

"O.K.," he said.

"Remember," said Atom Allen, "we're friends, to look at us."

They went out and got in the elevator.

The elevator operator pointed at the package.

"The esoteric, eh?" he said sourly.

"That's right," Rush agreed.

The operator said, "I looked in the dictionary. It says an esoteric is somethin' that's understood only by the specially initiated."

"Yep," Rush said. "Only by the initiated."

The operator scowled, "What kind of a damned gag is that?"

"As the initiation progresses," Rush said, "we hope to learn."

CHAPTER III

THE TRAIL OF NOAH

THEY WALKED OUT of the hotel like old cronies, went down the main street two blocks, and turned into a side street where the dust was ankle deep.

Atom Allen kept looking sidewise at Rush. Finally, he remarked, "You're a card. I don't quite make you out."

"I have complexes," Rush admitted.

"Eh?"

"They grow," Rush explained, "out of association.

"Association?"

"With things like—well—Noah, there, for instance."

"*Heh!*" Atom Allen said. "If you're tryin' to say this is a goofy business you're mixed in, you're wrong. You're dead wrong. It's sensible, and its danged serious!"

They came to a car, a long touring car with the top up, an ancient vehicle of an expensive and sturdy manufacture which, because it had high wheels that gave it clearance, was probably more efficient on the Arizona range than the newer types of automobiles.

Atom Allen put Noah in the back seat, then opened the front door and looked at Rush. "Get in and hang your head and arms over the door," he said. "And if you start kickin' me, I'll shoot your legs off."

Rush did as directed, and found that he was in a very awkward position indeed from which to start hostilities. The road got rough, and Rush, draped over the door, bounced up and banged his jaw on the car door. There was nothing much he could look at except the ground streaking past, and he had never realized that modern motor cars went so fast; he became convinced that the old touring must be doing a hundred, and twisted his head for a cautious look, but the speedometer only said fifty.

"Get back down here!" Atom Allen ordered.

Rush hooked his jaw over the door again. The wind shook his hair, rocks whizzed past his head, and tall cactus and sagebrush fled before his eyes. Some of it scraped the car sides.

"This cactus is liable to scalp me," he complained.

Atom Allen said, "Swell! Be a start for what I'm gonna do to you."

"What do you mean?"

"Brother," said the little man, "did you think you was gonna steal my wife and get away with it?"

"What you figure on doing?"

"I haven't thought of all the things yet," Atom Allen growled. "But what I'm savin' to the very last is this: I'm gonna cut you up in little pieces and see if you'll attract buzzards."

Rush got the unpleasant idea that the little man wanted to do exactly that.

They drove fast for a long time, and turned off the main road onto a trail that was two bad tracks over a worse range.

Rush objected about hanging out of the car door.

"Shut up!" the little man snarled. "I could blow your backbone in two and nobody'd hear the shots!"

There were no houses of any kind. There was giant cactus, prickly pear cactus, devil's-walking-stick cactus, jumping cactus and barrel cactus. There was mesquite, sagebrush and Spanish bayonet. There were red rock buttes. There was sand and white alkali. There was dust. There was not much else.

Either thinking or looking at the country seemed to make the little man madder and madder.

"Just make one move!" he gritted. "You wife-stealer!"

Rush was glad to see the *hoedag*.

HE WAS not sure that *hoedag* was the name for it, but someone had pointed out a picture of one of the things on a post card and informed him it was called, as nearly as he could remember, a *"hoedag"*; so he appended that name to it in his mind and thereafter never had reason to give the structures any other name.

If you wanted to be kind, you could say this *hoedag* was the shape of a beehive; but it was more the shape of the mud piles that muskrats throw up in lakes when they make houses. In fact, it had no shape; it was outwardly just a mound of mud and sticks with a hole at the bottom for a door, and another hole in the top for the smoke to come out.

It was the kind of a thing the Navajo Indians lived in during the winter, and went off and left during the summer.

Atom Allen stopped his car before the *hoedag*.

He said, "Get out—you wife thief!"

Rush was very careful to make no quick moves getting out of the car. Atom Allen's face was flushed, his eyes were hot, and he breathed through clenched teeth. He was the kind of man who could fan a fire in his own mind. From his looks, he had been fanning flame all the way out.

Rush looked at the *hoedag*.

Atom Allen said, "Didn't expect me in such a place, eh?"

"Didn't know what to expect," Rush said.

"Heh!" The little man made the word a nasty explosion.

Rush nodded at the *hoedag*. "It probably has its advantages."

"You bet it has," the small man growled. "Brother, I trailed Mat out to this district twice, and trailed Pat once, so I figured you had the layout out here somewhere. Fact is, I knowed dang well you did. It's sure a logical place for your layout. So I been camped at this place for a week."

"You been camped here for a week?"

"That's what I said! Ever since I trailed you out here from Los Angeles."

Rush said, "But I've never been in Los Angeles."

Atom Allen showed his teeth. "Hell you say!"

Rush tried to sound as earnest as he could.

"Mat and Pat might have been in Los Angeles," he said. "I couldn't say about that, because I don't know Mat and Pat."

Atom Allen growled, "Pal, that line won't get you nowhere."

"Who is Mat?"

"Heh!"

"Who is Pat?" Rush asked earnestly.

"Heh!" the little man snorted. "Pal, you slay me!"

"LOOK, MR. ALLEN," Rush said as convincingly as he could. "There has been a little mistake here. My name is Clickell Rush. I came to Flagstaff for a vacation, and used the name Thomas Gooch because I didn't want to be molested by a certain party."

"What certain party?" Atom Allen demanded, looking interested.

Rush said, "You wouldn't know the party. He's a bird who's been molesting me for some time. Matter of fact, I've never exactly seen him."

"Another guy whose wife you stole, huh?"

"I haven't stolen any wives. That's what I'm trying to tell you. I'm just a fellow in Arizona on a vacation, a chump who is probably half smart, or he'd have told you all this before."

"Just why," inquired the small man, "didn't you tell me before?"

"Curiosity."

"Eh?"

"I wanted to see what the funny business was all about."

"And now you don't want to see?"

"I've concluded I'd as soon stay puzzled."

The little man grinned widely.

"I will say," he said, "that you're the best damn liar I've heard recently. Now get down on your hands and knees!"

"But—"

Atom Allen growled, "I don't believe a word you said!"

"Now look—"

The small man cocked his big gun.

"Get down on hands and knees!" he said.

Rush sank to hands and knees. Sand was hot against his palms, and rocks hurt his knees.

Atom Allen backed to the car, reached in, and brought out the package that contained the hairless, sour-looking animal that was something like a cross between a rat and a rabbit. He removed the paper wrapping from the wire trap. The animal ran around, then sat down and panted.

Atom Allen clucked sympathetically.

"Poor Noah," he crooned. "Is you hot, baby?"

Rush said, "Mind telling me just what that hairless wonder is?"

The small man pointed his big gun at Rush.

"You stay on hands and knees," he said, "and crawl through the door."

Rush angled to the right to avoid cactus, then crawled to the hoedag door and through it into a surprisingly black interior that smelled of smoke, old cooked food, and men in need of a bath.

There were two of the men who needed baths. They stood as straight as they could against the *hoedag* wall, one on either side of the door. Rush saw their feet as he crawled in, decided it was no natural place for men to be standing, and kept on crawling.

Atom Allen crawled in behind him, and one of the men standing beside the door knocked Allen in the head with a club.

CHAPTER IV

MAT AND PAT

THE CLUB ON Atom Allen's head made a ripe sound; and Allen gave a spasmodic jump and jammed his face against the packed-dirt floor. The two men fell upon Atom and wrestled madly to get a rawhide rope looped about the small man's wrists before he could regain consciousness.

Rush got to his feet and watched the seizing of Atom Allen. On the theory that it was not his war, that Atom Allen was going to get the little end of it, and that the two strangers weren't interested in him—or they would have hit him before they hit Allen—he did nothing but look on.

It was a good fight. Atom Allen was dazed by the rock blow to the extent of being about half conscious, but he still had enough stuff to maul most of the clothes off the other two. Finally, they got him hog tied.

The two had not said a word.

They did not say anything while they stood back and one felt around in his mouth to learn whether he had lost any teeth, and the other got untangled from what was left of his shirt.

Rush saw that they were both long, sunburned men who had the kind of faces that would make an upright citizen feel uneasy. One had long red hair and the other had shorter red hair; one wore damaged khaki pants, and the other wore damaged blue pants. Otherwise, they were practically alike in appearance.

Looking at them, Rush thought of two peas out of the same pod. Then he decided two red gorillas out of the same cage was more appropriate.

One went over and picked up the wire trap containing the animal and held it in the sunlight, that slanted in through the door.

"Noah," he said.

"Hurt?" asked the other.

The first examined Noah.

"Nope."

"Sure?"

"Yep."

Rush, in a pleasantly interested voice, said, "Without straining my powers of deduction, I'll hazard the guess that you are Mat and Pat."

The two long, red-headed men with the bad faces looked at Rush. They looked him over thoroughly. Then they glanced at each other.

One pointed at Rush. "Who?"

"Dunno," said the other.

"Stranger."

"Yep."

Rush said, "On the contrary, gentlemen, I think I belong under the heading of an innocent bystander, or at least an uninformed bystander, being as I am in a confused mental state as to what this is all about."

The two redheads looked at Rush.

"Prisoner?" one asked.

"Yep," the other agreed.

They took out blue revolvers with long barrels and the one in the damaged khaki pants menaced Rush while the

other came over and searched. He came across the vest and
fiddled around with it, then looked at the other redhead.

"Bulletproof," he said.

"Off," the other directed.

"Can't."

"Why?"

"Locked."

They went into a period of grim silence over that. Then
one drew back and planted a terrific kick on that part of
Rush's anatomy located directly back of his stomach.

"*Ouch!*" Rush said.

"Up!" one redhead said.

"Quick!" said the other.

ONE OF the long twins herded Rush out of the *hoedag*, picking up the wire trap containing Noah as they went out. The
other twin shouldered Atom Allen, and came staggering
along behind. The man herding Rush did not say anything,
but gave orders by gesturing with his gun.

Rush was not enthusiastic about his change in captors.
Atom Allen had been violent only when he got to thinking
about his stolen wife. These long, rust-haired twins looked
as if they would get violent over nothing at all.

Having made no aggressive efforts up to this point, Rush
began to wonder if the lamb policy wasn't a mistake. When
he was involved in something mysterious, he liked to make
progress toward a solution. He had let Atom Allen make
him a prisoner; had let Allen take him from the hotel into
the desert; had let these fellows in turn make him captive—
all under the impression he was progressing toward a solution.

He had not resisted. He could have resisted. Without
flattering himself, the Gadget Man believed he could have
kept Atom Allen from making him a prisoner, and kept

from happening everything which had happened to him after that.

Rush had a scientific gadget for just about every emergency. With the gadgets, he could have kept all this from happening to him, if he had wished. He was beginning to think maybe it had been a mistake not to have wished.

The tall twins stopped outside the *hoedag* and looked at Atom Allen's car, and at each other.

"Car?" one asked.

"Fire?" the other suggested.

"Sure."

The twin herding Rush shot a hole in the car gasoline tank, then struck a match and tossed it in the gasoline dribbling out of the hole. Flame went *whoosh!*—and soon bundled the car.

"Walk!"

Rush walked. They went over a hill, then down into a little canyon where they had to brace their heels and slide, sending streams of dirt and pebbles scurrying ahead. Down the gully a hundred yards was a turn, and beyond this turn was a flat stretch of sand. On the sand stood four saddled horses of the motley-colored variety called calico, or paint broncs.

The red-headed girl was not wearing the mink coat now. **IT HAD** occurred to Rush several times that it was a mighty hot day to be wearing a mink coat. He believed that he now saw the reason for her wearing it. The red-headed girl was now clad in nothing except a garment which had been fashioned by cutting leg holes in a large grain sack, and fitting the top of the sack with shoulder loops made out of twine. She was barefooted.

She was also tied wrist and ankle with gray rawhide rope, which looked as if it had been snipped off the piece which Mat and Pat had tied Atom Allen. More of the same stranded rawhide held a wadded cloth in her mouth.

Her mink coat was tied in a wad on the back of one of the saddles.

Atom Allen stared at the girl. His eyes popped. He gave vent to assorted gasps and grunts, astonished and puzzled, and opened his mouth several times to say something, but never got it out.

One long red-headed twin untied the girl, then pointed at a horse.

"Ride," he said.

The girl could not get on the horse with her wrists tied. A twin picked her up and threw her into the saddle, and she could stay there. The twin then looked at Rush and pointed at another bronc.

"Aboard," he said.

Rush explained, "It is an error to infer from my cowboy accouterments that I can ride, for the garments were merely donned for the spirit of the thing. Everybody else seems to be wearing them."

"Up!" the twin said.

Rush got on the bronc. The paint horse took a deep breath, put his head down, and went through motions. The saddle horn wasn't there when Rush reached for it. The ground came up and knocked the breath out of him.

"I told you!" Rush gasped.

"Again!" the twin ordered.

Rush got on the bronc again. The horse astonished him by standing perfectly still.

ATOM ALLEN was lashed across another horse. The red-headed twins mounted. The whole group rode down the canyon about a mile, then climbed the steep sides of the gash.

The horses were now traveling over solid rock, which would not take tracks. The rock lasted for half an hour. Then they climbed steadily, stopping at times to breathe the horses. The air was very clear, the sun hot, the only life occasional buzzards which never came near enough to appear as anything more than black specks in the sky. One red-headed twin carried the wire rat trap which contained Noah.

Finally, they came to the prehistoric cliff ruin. The ruin was under a great overhanging cliff, and it was undoubtedly ancient, although the path by which they reached it had been dug quite recently. Stones set in mud composed the cliff dwelling walls; some of the poles which had supported roofs of the various rooms were still in place, but for the most part, the mud-on-brush roofs had fallen in.

It looked exactly like the pictures of the ruins in the American history books.

The ruin occupied about half the space under the cliff. The other half of the space was filled with woven-wire pens about a dozen feet square and neck high. The pens were covered over with woven wire.

Running around in three of the pens were animals that looked like Noah. The other pens were empty.

Rush was herded into a cliff dwelling room which had no roof, ordered to sit down, and his ankles were tied together with rawhide rope, and his wrists were tied to his ankles. It was not comfortable.

One long red-headed twin scowled at Rush, then glanced questioningly at the other twin, drew his hand across his throat and said, "*Geek!*"

"Easiest," he suggested.

"Later," advised the other twin.

They left Rush.

CHAPTER V

DESCENDANTS OF NOAH

RUSH ROLLED AND twisted and jerked until he decided he had never been tied tighter in his life. He had always heard that rawhide rope would stretch when it was wet, so he tied himself into a strained backward knot and tried to spit on the ropes and wet them; but it was difficult to expectorate from such a position, and he was too dry to spit anyway. If he could have perspired sufficiently to dampen the ropes, that might have helped, but he had apparently perspired himself dry.

He rolled over to the wall, maneuvered around, and managed to rub his chest against the wall. He fell over backward several times, rubbed skin off his chin and his nose, and finally managed to rub two buttons off the front of his brown shirt.

The buttons were large and thick.

He worked around until he had one button lying on the other, then managed to bring his bound heels down on both of them quite bard. There was a sput! and both buttons began burning with an intense blue flame. Rush jammed his rawhide bindings into the flame.

He expected to burn himself about as much as the ropes. He did. That was why he had tried to wet the ropes and stretch them. Pain of the burns made him grimace, hold his tongue with his teeth; he perspired all over.

After he had thrown the charred ropes aside and jumped about until the burns were not hurting as much, he went to the hole in the wall that served as a door and peered through. He saw no one. Intent listening convinced him the tall twins were in the vicinity of the pens. He crawled through the hole, sidled across several rooms and reached a point where he could see the pens.

The red-headed men were examining Noah with great care, pinching and pulling the animal, apparently to make sure he was intact. After they put Noah in the pen, they stood and watched him. It took fully five minutes to satisfy them.

One twin picked up an axe, the other a pail. Then they vanished down the cliff path, apparently after firewood and water.

It was beginning to get dark.

The girl was in the third cliff-dwelling room into which Rush looked.

RUSH UNTIED the girl and she said, "A fine damned detective you turned out to be, taking your damned time—"

"You must have been around that hotel clerk," Rush interrupted. "And what gave you the idea I was a detective?"

"Listen, stupid, they've got the animal back, and they've got—"

Rush said, "What put it in your head that I was a detective?"

"That's not important—"

Rush said, "You let me be the judge of what is important. Right now, first and foremost, I want to know how I got rung in on this jamboree."

"It was the Los Angeles Detective agency."

"The *what?*"

"The detective agency I called in Los Angeles," the girl explained "Mat and Pat have been keeping me out here. I didn't want to stay, so they took my clothes." She grabbed the coarse grain sack with both hands and held it away from her skin distastefully. "But I found where they had my mink coat hid. It was in this sack, and I made a pair of step-ins, or whatever you'd call this thing, out of the sack. I wanted to take all the animals away with me, so I found the rat trap. But I couldn't catch any of them except poor old Noah."

"You say a detective agency in Los Angeles—"

"I took Noah and escaped," the girl continued. "I wrapped the upper end of the sack around my feet, and after daylight, it wasn't so bad. I just walked in the places where there weren't rocks, and kept going."

Rush said, "I don't know any detective agency in Los Angeles."

"I found an Indian," the girl went on. "Me and the Indian done a lot of grunting at each other, then he took me into Flagstaff."

"If I did know a detective agency in Los Angeles," Rush said, "they wouldn't have known I was in Flagstaff."

The girl stood up. "Where's the boys?"

"If you mean Mat and Pat, they're out bringing in the water and kindling. Now, about this detective agency—"

"They'll kill you," the girl said. "They're mean. They're ornery as snakes."

"Listen," Rush growled, "I don't believe any detective agency told you—"

"They did too!" The girl frowned. "I called this agency because I'd used 'em one time when I thought the Atom was two-timing me. I was wrong about that. Anyway, I called the agency and told them my story. They said it was a very unusual story, and that they would call me back. Then they called back and said they'd consulted somebody who handled their unusual crimes for them, and that he had his stooge in Flagstaff and that the stooge was you and—"

"*Whoah!*" Rush said.

"Eh?"

"This Los Angeles detective agency consulted somebody who handles unusual crimes for 'em?"

"That's what they said."

"And I'm the stooge for this solver-of-unusual-crimes?"

"Yeah. That's what—"

Rush ground his teeth and stamped around in circles. **HE WAS** interested in Mat and Pat and Noah and the rest of this mystery. But he was about equally interested in this solver-of-unusual-crimes. For several months, he had been interested in the unseen individual.

It was several months ago that Rush had gone to New York City in hope of selling his crook-catching gadgets to the police force, and had failed. Then he came into his room one day and found a ridiculous-looking toad sitting on the table.

Inside the toad was a clever wired-wireless transmitter-receiver, and when Rush plugged this into the light socket, a voice somewhere in the city—he did not know where—told him of an unusual crime. Under the toad was half of a ten-thousand-dollar bill. Rush solved the crime. The other half of the bill arrived without comment.

Rush had never learned the identity of the voice of the toad. It was ridiculous. It was also annoying, because unusual crimes kept cropping up, along with halves of ten-thousand-dollar bills. Rush soon piled up a nice bank account, tried to quit solving unusual crimes—and couldn't. His fantastic, unknown employer kept shoving cases onto him. This one was an example—it had been shoved onto him. Rush had come to the point where he was very anxious to find the voice of the toad, after which he expected to put his best efforts forth in knocking the fellow's block off.

Almost everything about the voice of the toad was a mystery. Not the least mysterious was where the fellow managed to dig up such unusual crimes.

Rush stopped stamping around the cliff-dwelling room.

He snarled, "So the voice from that danged toad has got detective agencies scouting up crazy crimes for me!"

"Toad?" the girl said.

"Yeah—toad!"

"Mister," the girl said, "somebody must be crazy."

"I think he's crazy, all right," Rush growled. "Can you imagine a guy with more money than he knows what to do with, who amuses himself by standing on the side lines watching me solve unusual crimes for him? Sure, he's crazy! You bet he is!"

"Talk something that's sense," the girl ordered.

Rush nodded. "Let's talk about Noah and his descendants. Or is that sensible either?"

The girl said, "Atom and I had a farm near Los Angeles and were raising the animals. We had brought the animals up from South America ourselves."

"How'd they get here?"

"Mat and Pat," the girl said. "They stole every animal from the farm, kidnaped me so I wouldn't tell Atom, and brought us here."

"Mat and Pat were going to raise animals themselves, eh?"

"Exactly."

"What kind of animals?"

"Eh?" The girl stared at Rush. "You *must* be stupid!"

Rush said, "If not knowing what that Noah thing is called is stupid, then I'm it."

"They're chinchillas."

"Bugs?"

"No, no—chinchillas. You know—to make fur coats."

"Bugs it is!" Rush snorted. "Look—I never saw a chinchilla, I'll admit. But they've got *fur*, haven't they?"

"Sure."

"May I point out that Noah and his progeny are as bald as billiard balls?"

"Oh, that!" The girl shrugged. "They lose their hair when you first bring them up from South America. But the hair grows back in again."

Rush pondered. "I saw in a newspaper where a movie star paid thirty thousand dollars for a chinchilla coat."

"She didn't get a very expensive one, then," the girl said. "The chinchilla is practically extinct. These breeding animals are worth several thousand dollars apiece."

"You mean Noah is worth several thousand?"

"Of course."

Rush sighed.

"Let's drop Noah," he said. "Why didn't you report Mat and Pat to the police for kidnaping and grand larceny?"

"Those two no-accounts," Mrs. Atom Allen said, "are my twin brothers!"

CHAPTER VI

PEACE TO NOAH

RUSH PUT HIS head out of a hole in the cliff dwelling and saw no sign of Mrs. Atom Allen's red-headed brothers, Mat and Pat. He went to the cliff edge and looked over cautiously. He could search the path for a considerable distance down, but there was no trace of Mat and Pat.

The girl had found her mink coat and was putting it on, in spite of the warmth.

Rush asked, "Where did they put the Atom?"

"Over there." She pointed. "Only I don't think we'd better turn him loose."

"Not turn him loose? Why?"

"I'm afraid of what he'll do to Mat and Pat," Mrs. Atom Allen said in a frightened voice.

"You're afraid—" Rush swallowed. "Atom will take them apart, eh?"

"I—I think so!" The girl bit her lips.

Rush began grinning; his grin got wider and he felt very cheerful in spite of various aches and pains.

"Swell!" he said. "We'll turn Atom loose and sic him on Mat and Pat."

He walked over to the spot indicated by the girl as being the reposing place of her husband, and found a square hole with blackness below. He looked down into the hole, but it was too dark to see anything."

"*Ps-s-s-t!*" said a whisper in the hole. "C'mon down an' help me!"

That all whispers sound more or less alike was something that Rush did not stop to remember; and it likewise slipped his mind that Atom Allen had been gagged when last seen. It also did not occur to him that the long red-headed twins might elect to say more than one word at a time.

So Rush dropped into the hole, and was chagrined when flashlight glare splattered over him and two pistols jumped into the luminance, where he could see them.

After a moment, Rush discerned that the pistols were held by Mat and Pat.

Atom Allen lay on the floor, bound and gagged.

The red-headed twins blinded Rush with the light and gouged his ribs with the gun muzzles.

"Nuisance," one growled.

"Sure," the other agreed.

"Croak'm?"

"Lets."

RUSH KNEW he had better do something before they remembered he still wore the bulletproof vest, and took their guns out of his ribs and pointed them at his head.

Rush grabbed a gun wrist with either hand, and because it was foolish to think he could stand there and hold one red-headed twin with one hand and the second twin with the other hand, Rush ran forward. The twins were carried off balance. They galloped backward with Rush, hanging to their guns, trying to set themselves to twist free.

All three of them fell over Atom Allen. One gun went off with a deafening report. Rush beat that gun and the hand which held it against the floor until the gun flew off somewhere. That meant one twin was without a gun.

Because he had to let go of one twin or the other, Rush released the one who had lost his gun, and concentrated on the other.

With care and force, Rush managed to bump the armed twin with a shoulder. When nothing happened, Rush shouldered the twin again. This time the fellow yelped, and Rush knew the hollow steel needle mounted under the vest and projecting through the armor mesh when something hit over it with enough violence, had jabbed the man.

Rush shouldered him twice more for good measure—he wanted the needle to inject enough anaesthetic into the fellow to incapacitate him in a hurry.

When the twin began to weaken, Rush got the gun away from him. Rush fired the gun twice into the ceiling.

"I'll blow your heads to pieces!" Rush yelled.

Then he shot off the gun again with ear-splitting violence.

That was to intimidate the remaining twin, if he was susceptible to that kind of stuff.

Rush doubled over and charged through the darkest parts of the room, going football fashion, shoving out the shoulder which held the hypo needle that they hadn't found, because they had not been able to unlock the bullet-proof vest.

The other twin sidestepped Rush, kicked, and missed. It must have been a tremendous kick, because the twin's foot was higher than Rush's head when Rush heard the swishing sound and put his arms up protectingly and caught the foot by accident. Rush jerked, twisted. The twin made bull noises and came down. Rush got down with him and tried for several moments to shoulder the twin with the needle, and finally had to end it by bruising his knuckles on the man's jaw. The twin relaxed.

"Hey!" Rush called.

"You mean me?" the girl asked anxiously from outside.

"I'll pass 'em out to you," Rush said.

He pushed Atom Allen up through the hole, and the girl dragged the man the rest of the way. They got Mat and Pat out the same way, then Rush climbed out.

Rush untied Atom Allen.

Atom Allen got up, made a snorting sound, and grabbed hold of Rush. He grabbed hold confidently, in a way that showed he expected to bounce Rush around.

"Steal my wife, will you!" Atom Allen snarled.

He tried to pick Rush up. Instead, Rush lifted Atom Allen land tossed him against the nearest wall. Rush caught Allen on the bounce, held him up in the air, turned around and around until the Atom was dizzy, then slammed the mighty little man on the floor.

Rush said, "I took a lot from you in that hotel!" He picked the Atom up and bounced him off the wall.

The girl came over and kicked Rush's shins.

She screamed, "Why don't you pick on somebody your size, you bum!"

Rush got back out of her way.

The girl sank down and put her arms around Atom.

"Honeykins!" she gasped. "Don't you get it? The guy is a detective I hired."

Atom Allen considered that for a while, making thinking faces. Finally he put his arms around his wife.

"O.K.," he said, "if you say so."

"Love me now?" his wife wanted to know.

Atom gave that some thought.

"It'd be swell," he said plaintively, "if it wasn't for them dang brothers-in-law."

IT WAS after midnight, and Rush was trying to get the head of a Los Angeles private detective agency on the long-distance telephone.

A Flagstaff deputy sheriff put his head in the door and complained, "His wife talked 'im out of it. And now that Atom guy won't prefer charges against them red-headed twins."

"*Sh-h-h,*" Rush requested, listening to the telephone.

"It's all right, though," the deputy said. "We found out the twins are wanted for a little bank-robbing job in California. They'll get theirs."

Rush said, "Vamoose! Beat it! Shoo!"

The deputy said, "Oh, yes. There's a telegraph messenger out here with some money that's been telegraphed to you."

"Ten thousand dollars?" Rush asked.

"Yep."

"From somebody named Bufa?" Rush demanded.

"Uh-huh."

"Any message with it?"

"Yep. Message says: 'Sorry I wasn't there to watch it.' And it was signed, 'Bufa'."

"The toad!" Rush grunted.

"Toad?" the deputy looked puzzled. "What do you mean—toad?"

Rush said, "Get out of here! You'd just think I was crazy if I started explaining!"

The deputy growled, "I've got my own opinion about the state of your mind, anyway!" and stalked away with dignity.

After a while, a voice admitted over the telephone from Los Angles that it belonged to the head of the detective agency.

Rush identified himself.

"Look," he finished, "I want to know who it is that you're supposed to get in touch with when you hear about an unusual crime?"

"We never reveal the identity of our clients," the voice said.

"This is once you're going to break the rule."

The voice said, "That may be what you think."

"Now, look—"

"Goodnight," the voice said, and hung up.

Rush cracked the receiver on the hook, hurried downstairs, and confronted the hotel desk clerk.

"I want to hire a plane to get to Los Angeles!" Rush yelled.

"Then we'll get you a damned plane!" the clerk yelled back at him.

RUN, ACTOR, RUN!

THE GADGET MAN TAKES A PLANE TRIP—
AGAINST HIS WISHES—AND LANDS
ON A MOUNTAINTOP OF TROUBLE!

CHAPTER 1
TICKET TO TROUBLE

WHEN RUSH OPENED the hotel-room door, the messenger boy came in all bustling and important. He had an envelope.

"Here y'are," the messenger said rapidly. "Here's your ticket."

The messenger boy looked to be about fifty years old and he had a flowing beard about the color of a scrub mop.

Rush took the envelope and looked in it. There was an air line ticket in the envelope. The ticket entitled him to fly to Los Angeles on—he looked to see when—a plane leaving at three o'clock. That was in two hours.

This was very surprising because Rush had not ordered any airplane ticket to Los Angeles.

Rush said, "You sure this is for me?"

"Yep."

"You're positive there's no mistake?"

"Yep."

"And there couldn't be any mistake in any shape or form?"

"Nope."

Rush got out a five-dollar bill. He let the messenger see that it was a five-dollar bill. Then he folded the bill once lengthwise and twice across. He flipped the folded bill up in the air toward the messenger. The messenger reached for the bill.

Rush reached for the messenger. He got the messenger's wrists, wrapped one leg around the messenger's legs, and they fell on the floor. They wrestled around. The messenger looked old, but he was not old enough to be decrepit. He was a very strong man. He probably outweighed Rush by forty pounds, and felt as though he were made out of oak.

Rush was lean and wiry, and a little less than average height, out here in Arizona where there were lots of tall men. As he strained and struggled with the larger man, his neck and wrist sinews stood out like large bass piano strings, and bunching muscle bulged his brown coat in the

back. He got the big messenger spread out on the floor of the hotel room.

He searched the messenger's pockets, but there was nothing in the pockets except stuff that showed the man was an air line messenger.

Rush pulled on the beard for a while. It would not come off.

Rush got up, straightened his coat and yanked down his sleeves.

"Sorry," he said.

The messenger got up, made blowing noises through his nose, and felt of his beard.

"You nuts?" he demanded.

"That's it," Rush said. "Sort of a pity, too, isn't it?"

The messenger closed one eye and looked at Rush evilly with the other.

"What the hell was the idea?" he asked.

"Why, when I give a five-dollar tip," Rush said, "it always affects me that way. I have a kind of fit. I always grab people, and if they've got beards, I pull them."

The messenger unfolded the five-dollar bill and looked at it front and back, then put it in his pocket.

"Phooey!" he said.

He went out, slamming the door, and walked away with hard, stamping steps.

RUSH EXAMINED the airplane ticket again—he felt the need of being really convinced that it was made out to Mr. Clickell Rush. It was, with the name spelled correctly. Furthermore, it was one of those tickets with a form where the passenger's age, height, weight, and profession are all filled in. This information was all on the ticket, all correct, and all satisfactory to Rush—with one exception.

The exception was the designation of his profession. The ticket had been filled out:

PROFESSION—Fugitive.

"Fugitive!" Rush howled.

He had been under the impression he was a detective.

"Fugitive!" he gritted.

He began to itch mentally. He threw the ticket on the bed, got down on his knees beside the bed and dragged out a brown leather traveling bag. He opened the bag. All the clothes in the bag were brown; and all the accessories—the belts, the neckties, the socks—were shades of brown.

The toad was not brown.

The toad was Missouri-mud yellow underneath and swamp-moss green on the back, with warts. It was a large, fat toad made out of papier-mâché. Its mouth was open wide, as if it were about to get a fly or a bug or whatever toads eat; and its glass eyes had a big devilish gleam.

Rush put a lighted electric-light bulb in the toad's mouth, then stood back and waited. He began to look sheepish.

He always looked sheepish when he had to fiddle around with the toad.

IT WAS silly. It was so damned silly. Pretty soon the heat from the lighted electric bulb would cause a thermostat concealed in the toad's tongue to close, and that would switch on a compact wired-radio "transceiver" which the toad had instead of entrails, and it would begin to talk. It wouldn't talk, actually.

The talking would be done by someone else somewhere in the city, talking over another "transceiver" plugged in on the city lighting system. The toad just reproduced the other speaker's words. It worked like a radio—a two-way radio—for Rush could talk back to the other. He could say anything he wanted to say to the other, and that was some satisfaction; but it was still silly.

Rush never knew to whom he was talking. That made it worse. That was the craziest part of the whole unusual thing which had begun months ago when Rush invented several hundred gadgets for catching criminals—gadgets which he thought were very efficient, if fantastic.

He'd taken them to New York to sell them to the New York police force. The cops there had agreed the gadgets were fantastic. They hadn't thought the gimmicks were efficient enough to buy any of them.

Then Rush found this toad in his room—the toad, and a note telling how to tune it in, and a half of a ten-thousand-dollar bill. The upshot of that had been that Rush had solved an unusual crime for the voice of the toad, a voice that identified itself as Bufa, "which fed on slugs and snails—human variety."

For solving the crime, Rush got the other half of the bill; and that was nice. He had been shot at a few times during the solving of the crime—which wasn't so nice. Other crimes had followed for him to solve. And he had been shot at some more, slugged, chased, stabbed at, and he had decided, finally, that he didn't like the detective business.

For months now, Rush had been trying to escape from the unknown voice of the toad. Rush wasn't a detective who needed or wanted any more cases.

Rush was a detective who was trying to quit being a detective.

Maybe it was all very sensible, but Rush was willing to argue the point.

THE TOAD said, *"Hello."*

Rush jumped. Then he leaned over and began barking at the microphone which was concealed behind that part of the toad where ears should logically be.

"Look," Rush said violently. "I've got enough. I've had enough for months. I quit!"

"Heh, heh!" said the toad.

"Whatcha mean—heh, heh?" Rush demanded.

"Leff."

"Huh?"

"Leff. I'm leffing at you," the toad said. *"Like this: Heh, heh! Leffing."*

Rush clamped his lips, blew out his cheeks and overcame an impulse to heave the thing out the window.

"You're bugs," he said. "You're nutty as a peanut stand, or you wouldn't have thought up this fantastic business in the first place. But why not come out in the open once? Why not let me see who you are?"

Bufa, the toad, snorted.

"I'm afraid," its voice said.

"Afraid?"

"Sure. You bet you I'm afraid. I want to die of old age. I don't want crooks shooting at me. But I don't mind watching them shoot at other people. In fact, I get a big kick out of it. I get ten thousand dollars' worth of kick out of it every time it happens. Yes, it's very entertaining to watch you and the crooks tear into each other."

Rush was mad enough to feel like jumping up and down.

"What about me?" he yelled. "Do you think I get a kick out of it?"

"Sure," Bufa said.

Rush gulped. "Huh?"

"Sure, you get a kick out of it," the toad said. *"You may think you don't, but you do. I can tell from the way you go chasing around after the crooks."*

Rush shoved his jaw out at the toad.

"Look," he said, "this time is going to be different. This time I don't solve any crime for anybody."

The toad made a snorting noise.

"Now look," it said. *"This time you are going to have a very interesting affair with a movie actor who is—"*

"Listen," Rush said.

"What? What did you say?"

"Just listen," Rush ordered.

Rush picked the toad up carefully and set it on the floor. *"Listen?"* the toad said. *"What will I listen for?"*

Rush pulled up the right leg of his brown trousers slightly, so it would not hamper what he was going to do.

"Listen," he said. "Listen closely."

"I'm listening," the toad stated.

Rush kicked the toad. He kicked the toad like he had been wanting to kick it for weeks. He kicked it so hard he fell down.

He kicked the head of the toad clear back against the part of it that was nearest the floor when it sat down. He kicked the toad into a ball of papier-mâché, wires, broken glass, batteries. He did it all with one kick.

The wad of junk that the toad had become sailed away like a football. It hit the window, the window broke with jangling glass, and glass and toad fell to the courtyard below, where the hotel manager heard it.

Before long, the hotel manager was at Rush's room door.

"Look, friend," the manager said firmly, "we feel you should move. We feel you should move at once. We have noticed you acting strangely at various times. We—well—will you please move?"

Rush pointed at some bags. "You see those bags?"

"Yes."

"Well, they're packed."

CHAPTER 11

PLANE LUCK

RUSH LEFT THE hotel by way of the back door. The manager helped him carry his bags down. The manager looked after Rush, dusted off his hands, then closed the door, obviously pleased.

There was an alley. Rush walked down that and found the back door of a store, a clothing store. He went in, bought a new gray suit and put it on. Also a new black hat.

He wore his old necktie. It was brown, and not a very inviting brown. It was shiny, and looked a little as if some gravy had been wiped off its surface.

He also wore his own shoes with the gray suit. They were large, brown, comfortable shoes with rubber heels.

The store man let him use the telephone. Rush called the railroad depot.

"Train to New York.... Next one in twenty minutes, eh? Well, that's swell.... Fill out one ticket and one section reservation all the way to New York."

He hung up feeling quite good.

"You a New Yorker?" the clothing-store man asked.

"I'm going to be," Rush said.

Rush got his two bags and walked toward the depot. In a gray suit and the black hat, he did not look like Clickell Rush, the "Gadget Man." When he did not wear browns, it changed him.

He got approximately halfway to the railway station. By that time, his face was thoughtful, his mouth squirming around in thinking shapes. And his eye had a gleam.

Before he could help it, he turned to the right up a side street.

He made himself stop.

"Now, hell," he said, addressing himself, "what's got into you?"

This street led to the airport.

He turned around, said, "Boy, you don't care why he wanted you to take that plane. You don't care who bought that plane ticket, do you? Of course you don't." Rush walked firmly back toward the street that led to the depot. He took long steps and kept his jaw out. He tried to feel determined.

Right in the middle of feeling determined, he discovered himself stopped.

He said, "It's the railroad for you, boy!"

That didn't do any good. He stood on one foot for a while, then stood on the other.

"Damn curiosity!" he said loudly. He added, for his own benefit, "It kills more than cats."

No good, either. He tried to think of terrible things that could happen to him if he went on being Bufa's hired sleuth. He thought of himself lying in a long black coffin while six men stood around and drove nails in the lid. Probably nobody would send him flowers. He would die so young, too. Some undertaker would probably charge five hundred dollars for burying him—

"Bugs," he said.

This wasn't doing any good, either.

"Go on, boy," he said. "Walk toward that railroad station."

That was good for half a dozen steps.

He stopped again.

"Ah-h-h!" he said disgustedly, and surrendered.

He walked to the airport.

IT WAS a so-so airport. That is, there was a place for the planes to land and take off, and some buildings that were not so impressive. Three hangars and a waiting room.

Rush thought the hangars wouldn't interest him. It turned out differently. Because he saw the messenger.

It happened that the messenger was looking all around. He was wondering if he was observed. Rush could tell that. The man pulled his beard thoughtfully, then disappeared into the smallest of the hangars.

Rush went to the hangar. Getting near it, he lifted up on tiptoes so as not to make any noise. He looked in an open window.

The messenger was taking off his uniform. He stripped to his underwear. Then he took a bundle from behind some barrels, removed a blue-serge suit from this, and put it on.

He hid his messenger uniform behind the barrels.

It was the hiding of the uniform that decided Rush. That, and the fact that the messenger was furtive about it.

From a pocket, Rush removed an article which might have been a mechanical pencil, but wasn't. Except in looks. He pulled out the eraser end of the pencil. It proved to be a tiny pump plunger, working in the barrel of the pencil.

Rush aimed the point of the pencil at the messenger, pressed on the plunger, and a thin stream of liquid shot out. The drops struck in a gentle rain around the man's head and shoulders. Rush emptied the pencil barrel in one long push, and got most of the liquid on the man through the open window.

The fellow turned, feeling of the damp side of his face. Rush had ducked out of sight. The bearded man patted his damp coat collar, coughed. Coughed again. He doubled over with his coughing, then took hold of his throat and made amazing faces. He had a species of spasm, then tried to run for the door; but his legs gave out on him, let him down. He kicked a few times, then was still.

Rush ran around to the door and dived into the hangar. For several minutes he kneeled beside the messenger and watched anxiously. The anaesthetic; in older to work so swiftly, had to be strong; and sometimes victims had weak constitutions and needed a stimulant afterward. This one didn't. Rush hadn't thought he would.

In the pockets of the bearded man's blue suit was an airplane ticket. A ticket to Los Angeles, on the same plane Rush was to take. The ticket was made out to "John Smith."

His pockets also held a telegram—the lower part of a telegram. The address had been torn off. It read:

TAKING PLANE DUE IN ARIZONA TERMI-NAL AT THREE O'CLOCK STOP GET THIS MAN CLICKELL RUSH ON PLANE AND BOARD IT YOURSELF STOP I HAVE THE SPOOL STOP BOTH ACCOUNTANTS ARE ABOARD SO BE CAREFUL
A.A.

"That," Rush said disgustedly, "sure tells a lot."

THE PILOT of the plane was doubtful.

"The line has a rule," he said, "against taking drunks on our ships."

He was a tall, clean-chinned, determined-looking pilot.

Rush held the bearded man up with both arms.

"He's not drunk," Rush explained. "He just passed out for a little while. This sun doesn't agree with him."

The pilot frowned. "He looks to me like a hospital case—"

"Now, look here," Rush said. "There's going to be plenty of hell raised if you don't let us aboard this plane. My friend here will be as good as new in a short time. I'm positive of that. We've got important business to attend to, and if we miss this plane, somebody is going to get sued."

The pilot thought that over. He examined the bearded man, listened to him snore.

"Oh, all right," he said. "You've got tickets for this plane, I suppose?"

Rush said, "Both of us have got tickets."

The copilot helped Rush get the bearded man into the plane. The copilot was clean-chinned, too, but shorter, and had freckles. The hostess was not in sight, but Rush had seen her go off toward the waiting room. Their seats were toward the rear.

There were no other passengers in sight, but there might be some forward. The forward section was fitted with sleeper compartments that were little cabins to themselves, with an aisle through the center to the pilots' compartment.

The motors had not stopped. Now they speeded up. The hostess came running, climbed in and slammed the door. An attendant took away the stairs which were on wheels. The plane ran across the field, picked up its tail and took off. It was astoundingly quiet. Conversation in a moderately loud voice would carry from one end of the craft to the other.

The hostess came forward. Rush was unbuttoning the bearded man's collar and loosening his necktie, and when the hostess stopped beside them, Rush looked up.

The stark way she was holding her face startled him.

Rush said, "It's not bad enough for you to look that way."

The hostess had long brown hair which curled slightly at the ends. Her nose was long and finely moulded, and her mouth was a luscious, inviting, exciting, warm, soft, kissable cupid's bow. Her deep-brown eyes—they would have made Rush want to go swimming, if there hadn't been such terror in them.

She lifted one arm stiffly, with an effort, until it pointed at the bearded man.

"They—they sent someone to Arizona after him?" she gasped.

"Not that I know of," Rush said.

She swallowed. "Did they kill him?"

Rush said patiently, "He's not dead. He's only sleeping. He'll be all right."

"Oh."

"Who was going to try to kill him?"

"Why, the man working with the accountants—" She stopped and stared at Rush. "Who—who are you?"

Rush said, "Suppose you sit down here and tell me what this is all about."

When he saw she was not going to sit down, he reached for her arm. She jerked back. She was quick.

Rush got up out of his seat.

The girl's hand whipped into her uniform coat pocket. Suddenly, Rush was looking into the little black snout of a flat automatic she had produced.

"Sit down!" she said with a kind of desperation. "I'm going forward and stay with the pilot. If I see you coming, I'm going to shoot you in the legs!"

Rush sat down.

The hostess backed away, put her hand and her gun in her coat pocket, and kept on backing until she disappeared in the pilots' compartment.

"Where am I?" the bearded man wanted to know drowsily. "What's going on?"

Rush grumbled, "That's a logical question."

THE MESSENGER was lying back slackly in his seat. After a while, he began rubbing his face and working his fingers around in his beard.

"Sunstroke feel better?" Rush asked.

The bearded man blinked several times. "Sunstroke?"

"What else could it have been?" Rush inquired.

The man started scowling at Rush. "You knocked me out some way!" he accused. "What was the idea?"

"The idea," Rush said, "was that I got curious about why you were pretending to be a messenger. Can you explain?"

The whiskered man became astoundingly indignant at the question.

"I can't be mixed up in this, not publicly!" he snapped. "Think of my name! The public never understands! You get mixed up in anything, and they only see the dirty side. They'll think I'm a crook! I can't have that." He grabbed Rush's arm angrily. "Damn you, have you told anybody who I am?"

"Who are you?"

"Eh?"

"Who," Rush repeated, "are you?"

The bearded man's eyes became immensely relieved. "You don't know?" he demanded.

"Of course not."

"Then"—the man settled back—"darned if I ever tell you."

Rush tried glaring at the man, but that had no effect. The fellow obviously did not intend to talk. Rush considered. Finally, he got to his feet.

"Where you going?" the bearded man barked nervously.

Rush said, "To see if a girl meant what she said about shooting me in the legs."

HE WALKED along the aisle between the seats in the after part of the plane cabin. The ship was perfectly steady, and he could see forward along the aisle, between the little sleeper compartments, to the open door of the pilots' cockpit. Both the girl's shapely legs were visible, but none of her upper body. He reached the part of the aisle between the sleeper compartments.

"I wouldn't," said the man who stepped out of one of the compartments.

The man showed a gun. It was a deep-blue gun with a perfectly round pencil of a barrel about twelve inches long, and a varnished wooden grip like a large egg, a magazine that extended down in front of the trigger guard instead of fitting into the grip, as in guns of American make.

The man was tall, wide and as well-stuffed with fat as a sausage. He did not have pleasant eyes.

Rush looked at the gun. There seemed to be nothing to say.

"It probably wouldn't hurt much," the other grated. "I'd shoot your spine in two, and it would kind of paralyze you instantly. But the best way is to go back and sit down."

Rush returned to his seat. The man with the gun sat across from him and menaced both Rush and the bearded man with the gun.

A moment later, another man got out of one of the sleeper compartments. He was also fat, but not as large. More of a wiener.

He went forward to the pilots' room, took out a long-barreled foreign automatic of his own, and stuck his head and the gun in the cockpit.

A moment later, he tossed three automatic pistols back into the aisle. Two of the guns were big, undoubtedly had been taken off pilot and copilot. The flyers would carry such guns, because this was probably a mail ship. The smaller gun was the girl's.

After that, the plane began flying a different direction.

CHAPTER III

FORCED LANDING

FOR FOUR HOURS—RUSH sat all the time so he could see his wrist-watch dial—the plane flew on its new course. The man with the gun sat across the aisle and did not blink more than once every five minutes.

Rush said, "Mind telling me what we're in for?"

"Sure, I mind!" the man snarled. "Shut up!"

Having studied the fellow, Rush decided to let the subject drop. The man was on edge, as tight as a bowstring. He had thick lips, but there was nothing soft about them. They were ugly lips. His eyes were very small. He wore blue serge and his fat made it bulge at the thighs, shoulders, forearms.

It had been hot when they took off in Arizona.

It got cool, then cold. The air was difficult to breathe— easy enough to get in and out of the lungs, but without enough oxygen content to be satisfactory. They were high.

They flew into mountains. The mountains got taller, and snow appeared. A little snow at first, then a lot.

Finally, the only thing that kept the terrain below from resembling the polar regions was the fact that there were rocks and trees.

Rush said, "What I want to know is—"

The man across the aisle shoved his gun near Rush's face and pulled the trigger. The gun went off with ear-splitting violence. Rush thought he'd never had a feeling quite like it—that he'd been shot. Then he saw a hole where the bullet had gone out through the side of the plane. He wasn't shot.

"I told you to shut up!" the man snarled.

Rush sat very still. He was pale. His ears rang and rang.

The other man with a gun, the one who had been forcing the pilot to fly this course, came rushing back.

"What happened?" he barked.

He had thin lips for a fat man, and a beak for a nose. He was probably fifty pounds lighter than his partner, but still well-fed-looking.

"Nothing," the larger man said. "This guy just tried to talk."

The other man scowled at Rush. Then he spoke to his associate.

"We're over the cabin now," he said. "I'm gonna have the pilot land."

"Okay."

The smaller fat man went back to the pilots' compartment. En route, he picked up the three guns which had been lying in the aisle, opened a window and threw them over the side.

Rush judged, from the fact that the guns had been left lying there all this time, that there was no one on the plane but the pilot, copilot, stewardess, the bearded man, himself, and the two plump men who had the guns.

THE SPOT where they made the plane land must have been too small. At the last minute, the pilot ruddered the ship sidewise violently in an effort to kill air speed.

Evidently the pilot did not kill enough speed, for the plane hit, bounced, hit again, sloughed over, dug in one wing-tip. There was noise of a tin can in a shinny game with half a dozen clubs, only that sound was magnified.

As nearly as Rush recollected later, the plane turned once entirely over—wing for wing—and landed on its nose, then skewered around and flopped over on its back like a shot quail.

The cabin began to fill with smoke.

Rush did not recall becoming unconscious, but the next thing he knew he was hanging head-down from the safety belt, with warm crimson running out of his nose and getting in his eyes.

The smoke got worse.

He spent two or three minutes learning it was a trick to get out of a tight safety belt holding a man upside down. When he got loose, he fell on his head and shoulders. He said several words which fitted the situation, then saw the hostess in the thickening smoke.

The hostess was half in and half out of a narrow gap where the two sides of the plane had been mashed almost together. This narrow place was slightly aft of amidships.

The hostess was squirming, making agonized faces, twisting her arms and shoulders around. She had lost her neat hostess cap. Her hair was loose and its wealth emphasized her striking beauty.

Rush said, "Easy does it!"

He got down and put his arms around the girl in a nice way and began to pull to get her out of the narrow place between the mashed sides of the plane.

"Listen, stupid," the girl said, "I'm trying to get *in*—not out."

Rush changed from pulling to pushing. The girl disappeared through the crack.

Up forward, someone began swearing. Someone else was knocking against glass and cursing the nonshatter material used on airplanes, particularly in a window that would not open. The radio was still on, and working; and now that the motors had stopped, it could be heard.

The radio was saying something about visibility being fifteen miles somewhere—then a gun crashed twice. The radio became silent. A man—it was the one who had guarded Rush—said, "That fixed the radio so nobody will be telling anybody anything. If the plane burns, we're all set so no one will ever know."

The smoke was very thick now. There was coughing because of it. People moved around in the wrecked plane. They crawled and tore at things.

The bearded man's voice screamed, "The plane is burning!" He was up forward.

It was cold.

The hostess put her head through the hole. "Here," she said.

"What?" Rush got down close to her.

She gave him a spool of wire.

"Here," she said. "You keep this."

Rush held the wire, said, "Huh?"

"Keep that spool of wire," the girl said. "Hide it if you can. Because this whole mess is over that spool of wire."

Rush said another, "Huh?"

"Hide it, Gadget Man. Hide it."

THE GIRL was trying to crawl back through the crack. Rush got in front of her, blocked her way.

"Listen, you," the girl snapped, "the plane is burning!"

"So is my curiosity. You called me Gadget Man—how come you know me?"

"That," she said, "is something you can think about. Let me out!"

Rush said, "It strikes me funny you know me now."

"I figured out who you were."

"Now that spool— What—"

Rush squawked, "*Ouch!*" as she got him by the ears. She was strong. She twisted and hauled on his ears, as if she were a cowboy bulldogging a steer by the horns, and kept him so busy thinking about his hurting ears that she got herself through the narrow place. She went away in the smoke.

Rush listened. Flames made sizzling sounds. It was not as cold as it had been; in fact, it was getting much warmer.

Rush scrambled around in the smoke, hunting.

There was no trace of the bearded man—or anybody else.

"Does anybody need help?" he yelled.

A voice outside answered him. One of the men who had guns.

"Come outa there!" it advised.

Rush fumbled through his clothing and found cigarettes. The gunman had not taken those when he had slapped fingers over Rush, earlier, in search of a weapon.

Rush located enough fire to get the cigarette lighted. The forward part of the plane was burning violently.

He found a door, stepped through it into snow that was up to his waist. Smoke squirmed around him. He wallowed through the snow until he was out in clear evening air.

Evergreen trees stood all around, big, hardy trees, very green and pleasant-smelling, with their boughs laden beautifully with snow. The plane had broken off one of the trees—the impact must have crushed the cabin of the ship at the narrow point, where it looked as if it had been taken between a titanic thumb and forefinger.

Where the snow was shallow, it was about armpit deep.

"Won't you join the line?" asked one of the two men who had the guns.

BOTH THESE men stood to one side. The bigger one had, in some manner, ripped all the buttons off the front of his coat, vest and shirt during the crash, and he was using one hand to hold the garments shut over his fat pink chest, and only half succeeding.

Every one else who had been on the plane was lined up in the snow and the cold.

Rush got in the line—after he took note of what direction the wind was blowing.

"Anybody else in the plane?" he demanded.

The plane was a shiny metal monster which had folded its wings and taken on an uninviting shape.

"They're all out," said the small, wienerlike gunman. He looked at his larger, sausagelike partner. "I figure if we shot some holes in the other gas tank and threw a match, it would burn quicker," he said.

"Sure," said the large partner.

Rush had been smoking his cigarette violently. Now it sputtered very slightly. He took it from his lips, held it out away from his body.

The wind blew the cigarette smoke toward the two men with the guns.

One of the men coughed, squinted. The other started rubbing his eyes. He coughed, too. They both rubbed their eyes. Rubbed violently, in sudden agony.

Rush took long steps through the snow and got hold of their guns, one gun with each hand. He jerked. Yanked with all his force and got the guns.

He retreated with the weapons. To the girl, bearded man, pilot, copilot, Rush said, "Get back. There was tear gas in the cigarette."

They got back.

Rush's eyes watered for a while, giving him bad moments while he wondered if he had gotten enough of the vapor to blind him.

Feeling better, he said, "Those cigarettes finally did come in handy." He made his voice a violent yell for the benefit of the two watery-eyed, plump men. "Head for that cabin. Then everybody is going to tell secrets!"

CHAPTER IV

MOUNTAIN COTTAGE

THE TWO FAT men mopped their eyes out with snow and could see a little. They set off through the snow. The others followed.

Rush put a hand in his coat pocket as he walked and felt of the spool of wire. It felt like steel wire. Just plain steel wire.

No one seemed to have been badly damaged in the plane crash; but no one seemed to have escaped minor damages. Rush's nose still dripped.

They tramped through snow that was very soft and deep. They had to scoop snow out of the way with their hands, tramp it down, throw themselves sidewise at it.

The girl got close to Rush.

"You didn't hide the spool in the plane?" she whispered. "The heat would ruin it."

"No," Rush said.

"I hope you're not fool enough to still have it?"

"Sure, I have. What's foolish about that?"

"They'll just kill you for it if they can, is all," the girl said.

She fell back and Rush thought about what she had said. It didn't make sense. There was nothing about this that looked as if it would ever make sense. But it would; things like this always did in the end.

He put his hands up to his mouth, blew on them—
spurting breath-steam around his fingers—then beat them
against his chest, held them over his ears. He said, "Damn,
but my hands are freezing!"

That was the build-up. He put one hand in his pocket as
if to warm it, but actually to get the spool. He brought the
spool out palmed, then picked up a double handful of snow.

He made a snowball with the spool of wire inside.

He could hardly go around carrying a snowball and look
sensible. But he had a way to make it seem reasonable.

He used the snowball to stem his nose leakage. He
held the snowball against the back of his neck, also held
it between his eyes, and against the end of his nose. The
snowball got red and froze hard. Rush continued carrying it.

The leaders got in a drift, a very big drift; evidently it
filled a ravine of some kind, because all but Rush fell in,
some of them disappearing completely. They flailed around
and pulled each other out and went a different direction.

"Wait!" Rush yelled.

The whiskered man was no longer with them.

Rush plowed back to the snow-filled ravine.

"Come out of there, you with the whiskers!" he shouted.

There was no response.

Rush pointed one of his guns at the ground and pulled
the trigger. He pulled it again. The reports came jumping back from the surrounding peaks in a procession of
whacking echoes.

Before he could shoot a third time, a mop of whiskers
and a red, disgusted face appeared in the ravine, and the
owner climbed out laboriously.

"What was the idea?" Rush demanded.

The whiskered man licked his lips nervously.

"How's for lettin' me go?" he mumbled. "I've got enough of this."

Rush said, "Nothing doing."

"But my public—"

"Go on," Rush said. "Join the parade."

THE CABIN was made of logs. It was low and had a flat roof shingled with a foot-thick layer of sod. The builders had started off with one room and had added others. Evidently it was a job to pack window sash this high in the mountains, so the windows had been slighted. There was, judging from the number of chimneys of stone, a fireplace in every room.

At one end, the snow was deep enough to extend halfway to the roof. At the other end, it was over the roof.

Rush kicked the door open. Every one went into the cabin, and Rush pushed the door shut.

"You with the whiskers—you build us a fire."

The bearded man stamped the show off his feet and went over to a pile of kindling beside the fireplace. The others stamped snow off their feet also. They were all a little blue with cold.

Rush said, "Would somebody like to start explaining what this is all about?"

No one answered.

Rush said, "Line up against the wall. Pilot, you start tying them up—"

The bearded man turned around then and threw a stick of wood which he had been about to put in the fireplace. He threw the stick hard, and it hit Rush, knocking him off balance. Then the man charged at Rush.

The two plump men were faster. Together, they dived at Rush and got him before he could use his guns. They went down on the floor in a pile, and one of them used the stick of wood on Rush's head until the Gadget Man could no longer hold the guns.

Each fat man took a gun, took a few steps backward and menaced the group.

The bearded man looked utterly horrified.

He said, "I—uh—but I only wanted to get away from this terrible mess!"

"Shut up!" one gunman said.

"You done us a good turn," the other gunman told the whiskered man. "But we'd be glad to shoot you anyway."

The bearded man swallowed repeatedly and his hands trembled.

Rush looked to see if his snowball had burst in the fight. It hadn't. It lay on the floor.

"Make sure about the girl," one well-fed man ordered.

"Right," his partner agreed.

The man came over and peered closely at the girl. He moved his head from one side to the other to get different angles. The young woman eyed him coolly, her well-shaped chin up, a belligerent glint in her eyes.

That girl, Rush thought, was about the most striking bit of femininity he had ever seen.

Suddenly, the man grasped the girl's long brown hair and jerked it all off her head. Every bit of brown hair came off. It was attached to a make-up skullcap. The girl was a blonde.

The girl, with blond hair, was an entirely different person. She was changed. She was more vital, alive. She had been a striking girl before; she was remarkable now. Looking at her, Rush took in a deep breath.

The rotund man let out a pleased grunt.

"It's Ann Avon, all right," he said.

Rush thought so, too. She was Ann Avon, the motion picture star. Ann Avon, the latest sensation in Hollywood.

And Ann Avon, the reigning dollar-magnet at the box offices.

The fat men now went through a species of delighted tantrum. They stamped around and grinned from ear to ear.

"It's perfect!" seemed to be their refrain.

THEN THE men with the guns concluded to hold a conference over the new development, and ordered the others into a room of the cabin which had no window. The pair backed out, closed the door, leaving the prisoners alone.

Rush put his snowball down and jumped, got a grip on a ceiling beam, hung easily with one hand and tried to tear a hole in what looked like the most vulnerable part of the roof.

"If I can get a start," he grumbled, "I'll take a chance on either one of those fat boys catching me."

He had no luck with the roof. There were no windows. The only door was the one leading into the room where their captors were conferring. Rush picked up the snowball again.

He frowned at the girl.

"I don't see why the devil," he complained, "that you had to turn out to be a movie star."

She frowned back at him. "Why?"

"I was just making up my mind to see what I could do about liking you."

"And you wouldn't like an actress?"

"It's the other way around, I figure," Rush said. "An actress as famous as you wouldn't like me."

Ann Avon smiled.

"Maybe you just lack confidence," she said.

The bearded man held his head and glared at them.

"What is this?" he demanded sourly. "Such talk! Don'tcha know they're gonna kill us now?"

Rush looked at him with no approval. "What would you suggest doing about it?"

"I don't know," the man said with loose-lipped misery.

"For an air line messenger," Rush said unkindly, "you're a lot of help."

THE GIRL started. She fixed her eyes on Rush, but she pointed at the man with the beard.

"Messenger—him?" she said.

"Why yes. He started out as one."

The girl eyed the whiskered man, puzzled. "Lonny, you were never a messenger, were you? You were born wealthy, I thought."

Rush yelled, "What is this? *What is he?*"

"I'm Lonzo McGillicuddy," the bearded man explained drearily. "I'm a film comedian. I acted in such pictures as—"

"Never mind," Rush said. "I know the name. If you'd come out from behind the alfalfa, I might know your face. You're almost as big a name at the box office as Ann Avon, here."

Lonzo McGillicuddy said sadly, "I grew this beard for my latest picture." He added miserably, "This terrible thing will get in the newspapers and—"

"*Sh-h-h,*" Rush said. "Your public. We know."

Rush pointed at the pilot and copilot. "You actors, too?" he demanded.

The pilot shook his head. "I only fly airplanes for a living."

"I fly 'em, too," the copilot said. "That is, I sit and watch him fly 'em," he added, pointing at the pilot.

"Do you know what is behind this dizzy mess?" Rush asked.

Both airmen shook their heads.

"Would you like to know?"

Both airmen nodded.

"So would I," Rush said. "What do you say we take these two movie actors and start bouncing them off the walls until we get satisfaction?"

The airmen both looked horrified.

"Oh, you're movie fans!" Rush said sourly. His voice got loud. "Well, these two may be film big shots, but any time they think they can lead me around in the dark by the nose—"

The girl interrupted.

"Listen, noisy," she said. "You're supposed to be Clickell Rush, the Gadget Man. A man with a reputation. What about that? Did you get that reputation standing around barking at people?"

Rush looked indignant.

"Say, what do you expect—"

The door opened and both fat men stood in the portal holding their guns.

"Come back in this room," the first one said.

"We got a love feast all cooked up," the second one added.

CHAPTER V

THE LOVE FEAST

THEY FILED OUT into the other room and stood in a semicircle in front of the men with the guns, as they were ordered to do. The fireplace was full of leaping flames and warmth was rolling out into the room.

Rush glanced uneasily at his snowball.

The snow which had fallen into the room when they had opened the door was beginning to melt on the floor. Rush pointed at the snow.

"Look," he said. "We don't want it all wet in here if we're gonna have to stay here some time." He pointed at a corner. "There's a broom over there. How about me sweeping the snow out?"

The well-fed men looked at him.

"Go ahead," one said.

The other began, "But—"

"Let him sweep it out," the other said sharply.

Rush got the broom, opened the door, tossed his snowball into the snow beside the door where it would stay frozen. He swept all the snow out carefully, knocked the snow off the broom by hitting the broom against the side of the door, then closed the door and put the broom back in the corner.

"That's better," he said.

One fat man said, "Yep, I think it is." He was the larger of the pair. He turned to his companion. "You keep 'em here," he said. "I'm gonna go have a look at the plane and if the fire has burned out, I'm gonna see if I can find that spool of wire."

"Go ahead."

He went out, after turning up his coat collar. Cold air stopped rushing in when he closed the door.

The other man sidled to a cupboard. He got out a box of raisins. The raisins were frozen solid. He peeled the paper off them and began to gnaw. He chewed and looked at the others.

"Relax," he said. "Just relax."

They didn't feel like relaxing, or at least Rush didn't. He saw the bearded messenger-detective-actor eyeing him.

Said the fellow through his beard, "I thought you knew the whole story!"

He sounded quarrelsome.

"What gave you that crackpot idea?" Rush demanded. He sounded just as quarrelsome.

"WELL," **SAID** the actor, "when Ann Avon wired from New York that she was taking a plane, and she was afraid they would try to stop her, I got busy. Miss Avon said she was disguising herself as a stewardess, but she was afraid it wouldn't work. She was worried. She wanted a detective to meet her and guard her. So I went to a Los Angeles detective agency to get a man."

"You didn't hire me through any Los Angeles detective agency," Rush said.

"I sure did."

They glared at each other.

"All right," Rush said. "We won't argue. You didn't. You couldn't. Anyway, nobody hired me."

The part of the actor's face not covered by whiskers looked indignant.

"I did," he insisted. "I went to this Los Angeles agency, and they had a powwow among themselves. They telephoned somebody. I think the somebody was the cause of them telling me to go to Arizona and hire you and get on the plane with you when it came through."

"Did they telephone a party who called himself Bufa?" Rush asked.

"Who?"

"The Los Angeles detective agency! Did they—"

"I don't know who they called."

"It must have been the toad," Rush said.

"The what?"

"The toad."

The actor put his fingers in his beard and looked miserable.

"You're crazy," he said. "I knew you were nuts. The trouble with me is that I should have known when the detective agency told me not to let you know who I was, that you were bugs. The whole thing was whacky whenever it referred to you. Even the ten-thousand-dollar bill they gave me to give to you when you had solved—"

"Where did they get the ten-thousand-dollar bill?" Rush demanded.

"From the person they telephoned to, I gathered. The party you call Bufa, or toad, or whatever—"

Their guard put down his raisins and looked interested.

Rush said, half to himself and half to whoever cared to listen, "I been wondering where this Bufa individual digs up the queer crimes he shoves onto me. Now I know he's got private detective agencies hunting them for him. That private detective agency must know who Bufa is."

Rush put out his jaw irately.

"Just wait'll I get hold of this detective agency!" he yelled.

The man who had been eating the raisins came over and glowered at the bearded actor.

"Did I hear something about a ten-thousand-dollar bill?" He drew back his fist threateningly. "Where is it? Save trouble, pal. Tell me where that frogskin is!"

The actor sighed resignedly. "In my shoe," he said. "The right shoe."

"Take it off."

He took it off. The raisin-eater took the bill out, eyed it admiringly, folded it, put it in his own pocket.

"Nice piece of velvet," he said.

The actor looked at Rush. "Go ahead. Settle this. You gotta, now, to collect your pay."

The fat man had started back to his raisins. He stopped and pointed his gun significantly at Rush.

"You thinking about settling it?" he asked violently.

"Have I said anything?" Rush demanded.

THE PLUMP man who had gone away came back. He was glowing from the cold. Also from satisfaction.

"Nice," he said. "Mighty nice."

His partner eyed him. "All okay, eh?"

"Sure. We can tie them up now." He put his hands close to the fire. "I don't know whether we should just throw them out and let them freeze to death. Maybe it ain't cold enough. Maybe we should just bump their heads." He looked hopefully at his associate. "It's logical they would get their heads bumped when the plane crashed, ain't it?"

"We could shoot them," said the other.

"And maybe leave a bullet hole to be found in one of their bones? No good."

"That's right."

The man who had been out in the cold got his hands warm. He went prowling around the cabin. Obviously, they had been at the cabin before, and knew its layout and what it contained. The man located two five-gallon tins of gasoline.

"We should have more gasoline," he complained.

His partner frowned. "You don't think that is sufficient to burn the bodies enough to make it look like they burned up when the plane crashed?"

"Well, I don't know. But I hope so."

Rush looked at them blankly. "You figure all of that is necessary?"

They nodded.

"And," Rush said, "you think you'll be able to sleep after you do it?"

"Better than we would if we didn't," one large man said. "I been in jail before. You don't sleep so good in jails."

"Jails?" Rush said.

"It's this way," the well-fed man said. "Our boss has been looting a movie company and we been putting our noses in the trough with him. It's the old falsification-of-accounts gag that the bank cashiers use. The boss made it work because he also owns the firm of accountants that audits the movie company books. We're the firm of accountants."

"Oh," Rush said. "Somebody has been taking money from a movie company."

The man nodded at Ann Avon.

"She owns most of the stock in the company."

"You thieves!" the girl said angrily.

The man grinned at her sourly.

"You're slick," he said. "You sure can act. When you came to New York and told us the boss had sent you, you did such a good job that we spilled the whole gag. We emptied the works."

"And got it recorded," the girl said grimly.

"Yep. On a wire."

Rush said, "Wire—wire? Oh, I get it." Rush looked at the girl. "You used one of the new type of dictaphones that records by putting varying magnetism into a steel wire. The recorder magnetizes the wire. The transcriber is affected by the magnetism as the wire runs through it, and the impulses are stepped up in an amplifier and put out in a loudspeaker. I've got one of them things."

The girl, not looking at Rush, said, "Evidence enough to convict these men and their boss—he's a movie executive in Los Angeles."

"Then," Rush said, "they'd like to find the spool of wire."

The fat man who had gone out to look at the plane now laughed. He laughed loudly.

He took the spool of wire out of his pocket.

"We've got it," he said. "I found it in that snowball you tossed outdoors."

RUSH JUMPED at the man who did not have the snowball. The man had his gun pointed at Rush's chest. He pulled the trigger. The bullet hit Rush squarely in the chest.

Rush went up straight, threw his hands high as if clutching at something, and fell flat on his back. He turned over instantly and doubled up, doubled up completely so that his hands clutched at his shoes. Coughings, gurglings and hackings came out of his mouth and nostrils.

"The crazy fool!" said the man who had shot Rush.

Rush went on convulsing, his hands clawing at his shoes.

The other well-rounded man picked up a heavy stick of fireplace wood.

"I might as well put him outa his misery," he said.

He came over and raised the stick.

Rush got the heel off his right shoe, got what he wanted out of the hollow heel of the shoe.

Rush then straightened out violently and kicked the feet out from under the man with the stick. The man sat down so hard the floor made cracking noises.

The other round man seemed amazed. He must have had a lot of faith in his gun. He had shot a man with it, and it didn't seem to have damaged the man much. He ogled the gun for a moment, instead of shooting Rush again. He seemed to distrust the gun. That gave Rush time.

Rush raked a little lever on the thing he had taken out of his heel. He dropped the object. It was about like a safety box of matches, only flatter. It was black, but it burst open at one end and went into action.

First, it was like an electric sparkler, with bluish sparks. More sparks flew. Then flame. Flame rushed out of the thing. Blue, intense flame. Like the arc of a welding torch. A very large torch.

The flame became utterly blinding.

Rush got up and put his necktie—the ugly, shiny brown one that looked as if soup had been wiped off it—over his eyes. He held it over his eyes with one hand. The tie was made of a cellophane yarn impregnated with the proper dyes and chemicals, and it was a good-enough filter for the light wavelengths from the flame which hurt the optic nerves the most. He could see.

No one else could see as long as they looked toward the flame.

RUSH KEPT between the flame and the gunmen, picked up the stick of firewood and jumped to one gunman. He spent an instant wondering how hard he could hit without smashing a skull, decided it wasn't too important, and hit a blow that wouldn't be too light. The man fell.

The other man began shooting. He was trying to look through his fingers and see something. Evidently the fingers did not help, because he started shooting at the table under the impression it was a man.

The bearded actor suddenly emitted a bawl of fright. His nerve had held up well, considering. But it was gone now. He made headlong for the door, and the fact that he found it indicated he must have had the possibilities of the door in the back of his mind for some time.

He got outside and went away through the snow, most of the time on all fours, something like a torpedo.

Rush reached the second gunman with the stick of wood. He struck. The wood hitting the man's head made a drum-tap sound. The blow had no appreciable effect on the fat man, except that it caused him to jerk his gun toward Rush. Rush hit the gun hand with the stick of wood. He broke the arm, Then he hit at the man, but missed.

The fellow had whirled, was running. He ran wildly and blindly and headlong into the wall. His head made a loud bump on the wall, and he dropped on his face. Rush went over and hit him with the stick, decided that one wasn't hard enough either, and hit him again.

Then Rush ran outdoors and took the necktie away from his eyes.

The actor with the whiskers was tearing a gully through the snow.

"Hey!" Rush yelled. "Hey, you! Come back here!"

The actor was blinded, probably had his ears full of snow, and he was also scared. He kept going. Faster, if anything.

"Run, actor, run," Rush said disgustedly.

MAKING GAGGING sounds, Rush sank down in the snow beside the door. He held his chest, clawed at it with his fingers, and began to cough. His coughs were short, staccato, and continuous. He didn't seem able to manage a big cough. He tried and tried for a big cough, finally got enough air in his chest for it, and let fly. He became calmer.

Looking anxious, he took off his coat, ripped open his vest, making buttons fly. He was more careful with his shirt, remembering the cold. His bulletproof vest had a zipper and a trick lock. He got it open.

He stared, horrified, at a bullet hole in his chest.

He was still sitting there when the incredible blue light burned out inside the cabin; was sitting there when the girl came feeling her way blindly out of the cabin.

"I've been shot!" Rush croaked.

"My eyes!" the girl screamed. "I'm blinded! I can't see!"

"You'll get over it in an hour or so," Rush said hollowly. "But me, I've been shot."

The pilot and the copilot came out of the cabin. They must have had their arms over their eyes, because they were not as blinded as the girl. Their eyes streamed, but they could see.

"I'm shot," Rush explained.

The pilot said, "Damned if I can see why you're so surprised. You walked right into his gun."

The pilot then got down on his knees beside Rush. He seemed to know something about such things. He snorted. Then he laughed.

"The bullet is lying on your rib. I can squeeze it out with my fingers." He grabbed Rush suddenly, shoved him down, got on his chest and worked with his fingers. Then he stood up holding a malformed blob of lead. "See," he said. "There it is."

RUSH GOT up feeling much better, but looking sheepish. He put on his shirt, vest and coat, then picked up the bulletproof vest, which he had not donned, and drew back and threw it as far as he could out among the evergreen trees.

"I've got to invent a better one than that," he said.

He walked into the house, searched in the unconscious well-fed men's pockets until he found all their weapons. Also the ten-thousand-dollar bill. He pocketed the latter.

Carrying a pair of skis under one arm—the skis had been standing in a corner; no doubt the gunmen had intended to use them in escaping—Rush went outside again.

He handed the guns to the pilot and copilot.

"Could you shoot either one of the bologna boys if they wake up and start something?" he asked.

"I may shoot 'em before!" the pilot said violently.

"Swell. All right by me." Rush began putting on the skis.

"Where you going?" the pilot asked.

"After that actor," Rush explained.

"But he's not one of the crooks."

"He could freeze to death, though," Rush said.

"Maybe he'll come back."

"You can't tell about a scared actor," Rush said. "I'm going after him."

He took two or three confident, sliding steps with the skis, but they went different directions and he fell down in the snow.

"Bring me the two poles that go with these things," he said grimly.

They brought him the usual short poles with the little wheel jiggers on the ends.

"I can't have that actor freezing," Rush said. "He's got to show me the detective agency he went to. And that detective agency is going to tell me the name of that Bufa, the party who gets me in these messes." He looked at the others as if it might be their fault. "I've had about enough of such stuff as this!" he yelled.

He got under way.

A MAN AND A MESS

CLICK RUSH IS THE MAN, AND WHAT
A MESS HE GETS INTO WHEN HE
TRIES TO LEARN WHO BUFA IS!

CHAPTER I
THE MAN

THE HALL WAS long and had a plain tiled floor and naked plaster walls. There was a window at one end which looked out against a blank brick wall, but no window at the other end. The elevators, three, were located about halfway down the hallway. One office door was directly in front of the elevators, and lettering on this said:

CONTINENTAL DETECTIVE AGENCY
LOS ANGELES BRANCH

Clickell Rush opened this door and walked in, looking as important as he could.

Rush said, "I want to see the head man."

In a little while a man came out of an inner office. He was a wide fellow made of jaw, neck, arms, fists.

"Hello," he said. "I'm the head man around here."

"I'm Clickell Rush," Rush said.

"Well, well."

Rush said, "I want to know the identity of a party who goes by the name of Bufa."

"So you're Clickell Rush," the head man said. "My!"

He took both of Rush's hands and began shaking them heartily, holding the hands tightly, making great, shaking motions, up and down, and from side to side, until Rush was stumbling around, off-balance and trying to get loose.

"Get 'im, boys!" the head man called.

Four men came through a doorway. One man tied himself around Rush's legs, two men anchored to Rush's arms, and the fourth man went to the stenographer's desk, got out a rag that looked as if it were used regularly to clean typewriters, and stuffed the rag in Rush's mouth, fastening it there with some adhesive tape of the black, bicycle kind.

"*Urk!*" Rush said.

"I agree with you," the head man of the detective agency said. "You must be embarrassed. I know I would be."

Rush honked his rage through his nose. He put forth a succession of body convulsions during which his coat sleeves split over the biceps muscles, and the button flew off his shirt collar as his neck got many sizes larger than

normal. The antics got him nowhere. Finally one sleeve
came entirely off his right arm—both coat and shirt sleeve.
The arm was revealed as not large, but incredibly sinewed
with what could have been steel wire.

"Hit 'im with somethin'!" one man croaked finally. "We
ain't—gonna—be able—to hold 'im!"

The head man got out a blackjack. "This wasn't part of
the bargain," he said.

He hit Rush.

Rush stopped struggling. He wasn't senseless, or help-less, or even dazed. He just saw that the sensible thing was to stop struggling.

"The hearse will be around to the back door," the head man said. "We'll take 'im down there."

Rush gurgled around the gag. He wanted to know if they were going to kill him—and the noises he made left no doubt about what he was trying to ask.

"No, we're not croaking you, exactly." The head man pulled at his square jaw, rubbed his thick neck, then shook his head from side to side, and made a sympathetic cluck-ing.

"I'm afraid it may be worse than that," he said.

THEY REALLY put Rush in a hearse. It was a deep cloud-gray hearse with a lining of satin, colored the most depress-ing blue Rush had ever seen. One man sat on Rush's knees, another sat on his hips and a third on his shoulders. Drapes inside the windows had been pulled together, so no one could see them.

While the hearse rolled swiftly through Los Angeles streets, Rush had time to get an aching in his muscles, and to think. The thing that had happened to him was too astounding to make sensible thinking.

Just to get it straight in his mind, he took a mental review of what had led up to it. He—Rush—was Clickell Rush, inventor of scientific crook-catching gadgets, and hence known as the "Gadget Man." For months, he had been hired by somebody he'd never seen, somebody he knew only as "Bufa," to solve unusual crimes.

Bufa was a toad. More explicitly, Bufa was a voice out of a toad. The toad was artificial, big, and contained a wired-wireless "transceiver" and the voice had always come from another "transceiver" sending from spots unknown—

there was no way of tracing a wired-wireless "transceiver" with direction-finders.

Rush had grown very disgusted with being a fantastic kind of detective. When he'd tried to quit, Bufa had forcibly involved him in more unusual crimes. A few days ago, Rush had finally kicked the artificial toad part of Bufa to pieces, and now he was looking for the owner of Bufa's voice.

He'd heard that the Continental Detective Agency, Los Angeles Branch, had supplied Bufa with unusual crimes. Bufa was queer that way. He had apparently hired Rush for no other reason than that he got a great kick out of reading in the newspapers how Rush had solved the crime. Privately, Rush thought Bufa must be crazy. Personally, Rush wanted to find the guy and knock his block off. He'd gone to the Continental Detective Agency to demand Bufa's name.

And here he was. In a hearse. Three men sitting on him.

The boss detective—the one who admitted he was the head man—squatted down beside Rush and made sure Rush's gag wasn't choking him.

"If anything like this happened to me, I'd think somebody was crazy," the man told Rush. "But you—I guess you're used to it."

Rush was purple from not getting enough breath.

"You being the famous Gadget Man," the other said, "queer things are nothin' new to you."

Rush almost blew his eyes out trying to say what he thought about the whole thing.

Now he was no longer seeing the tops of downtown buildings through the hearse windows. The hearse traveled fast along boulevards where cars made zoop! noises in passing— Later, there were rolling hills, and the air had the clean smell of country.

The boss detective laughed and gave Rush a poke in the ribs with a thumb.

"You enjoy the country, I hope," he said.

The tires bumped over chugholes in a dirt road, then the hearse turned sharply right onto a very disused road where grass and short brush kept scraping the underside of the chassis.

"Well, here we are," the driver called.

The hearse stopped.

The head man opened the rear of the hearse and got out. "Stick here," he said. "I'll take a look at the cistern before we put him in."

RUSH LIFTED his head and saw the man walk to an old wreck of a house which had no windows, and only half a roof. The man stopped in the weeds in front of the house, moved some boards which were lying on the ground, then got down on his knees beside what must be the cistern. When he came back and got in the hearse, he looked pleased.

"The sides are too slick for him to climb out," he said. "And there's only about three feet of water in the bottom."

Rush made a loud, anxious noise around the gag.

The head man bent down and removed Rush's gag. They all waited for Rush to say something, but Rush glared at them without words.

A man asked, "How'll we break his legs?"

"We can run the hearse over 'em," the boss said.

Rush's knees began to knock together, although he had not been looking scared.

"Yonder is a rut we can lay his legs across," a man suggested. "We can hold 'im, while the hearse runs over his legs."

"Ho-hum," the head man said.

"Ho—what?"

The head man opened his mouth, yawned, patted his lips with the back of his right hand.

"Ho-ho-ho-hum," he said. "Guess I didn't get enough sleep—"

Then he lay down on the hearse floor and began snoring.

A man gasped, "What the—the—say—say—"

The three men sitting on Rush dropped their chins on their chests, loosened their bodies, and apparently slept. One of them rolled off Rush, but the other two remained sitting slackly on him. Rush heaved up and got that pair off his chest. Each of the four men was as loose as a sack of moles.

Rush rolled around on top of the men, fingers tearing and feeling, until he got a gun off one of them. He rolled with the gun to the rear door and fell out onto the weed-covered ground.

The driver bounded from behind the wheel and came running to see what had happened. He stopped, put his hands as high as he could.

"That's the idea," Rush said.

It was hard to lie on his stomach, twist his head around, and point the gun at the driver while his own wrists were tied together at the small of his back.

The driver strained so to put his arms higher in the air that he trembled.

Rush said, "Knock a window out of the hearse."

The driver pounded one of the glass windows out. Following more orders, he selected a jagged fragment of glass, wedged it upright in the earth, stepped back and held his own hat over his eyes. Rush sawed himself loose on the glass edge.

Rush saw one trousers leg was red, damp below the knee, and pulling it up, found that his knee, where the anaesthetic gas container fitted—the container was molded in sponge rubber and stuck in place with adhesive and was unnoticeable—had been cut when he broke the glass gas cartridge in the container by knocking his knees together, thus releasing the gas that had overcome the private detectives. It was not a deep cut, he learned.

Rush limped over and took a blue revolver, a blackjack and a private detective's badge from the hearse driver. The man was round, his face florid. He looked about as worried as possible, considering how difficult it is for a fat man to look worried.

Rush said, "Go over and lie down in front of the hearse. Put your legs across that rut."

The driver's mouth turned into a round hole with horror all around it. He said, "You—uh—uh—"

"Yeah," Rush said, "you're a good guesser."

The man said, "No—sake don't—" and some more, but the most of what he was trying to say, whatever it was, just came out of his mouth as terrified hisses.

"Then talk me out of it," Rush suggested.

"Uh—talk?"

"Sure. Start off with the hearse."

"Why, it's my hearse," the man said in a hasty, frightened voice. "My brother is the head man of the detective agency, and he just asked me if he could use my hearse. So I said, 'What the hell, you're my brother. Why not?' And so we did, on account of my brother didn't have nothing else suitable."

"I see."

"I really didn't want—"

Rush said, "Make me see more."

A gun banged. Rush jumped a yard—and no longer had the revolver he had been using to menace the fat man. Because a bullet had knocked the gun out of his hand.

"You get the idea," a woman's voice said, "that Icky can handle a rifle."

CHAPTER 11

THE ANGRY ARTIST

RUSH STOOD VERY still, only turning his head enough to watch Icky come out from behind a bush. Icky was small, twentyish, brunette. Not bad, either—except that she was marring her looks by shoving her lower lip out and up so as to look fierce. Her rifle was a brand-new auto-loader that the sporting goods catalogues recommended for elephants.

She said, "Look at the sun!"

"I'm—"

"Look at the sun! Do you want Icky to shoot?"

Rush looked at the sun, pinching his eyes shut tightly, and was completely blinded by sunlight whenever he tried to see anything. He felt the girl's hand search him quickly, and realized that she knew the places where men carried guns.

Next, she searched the hearse driver.

Then she hauled the four men out of the hearse, ordering each one of them to, "Wake up!" in a tone that grew more and more puzzled.

"Now isn't this one for the fools!" she said angrily.

Judging from the sounds, she slapped the men, and expended some useless time kicking them in the ribs and ordering them to get up.

"Well, two will do!" she said finally, and prodded Rush with her rifle muzzle. "This thing will shoot through two men as easy as one," she advised him. "So don't try using your friend for a shield."

"Look, lady," Rush said, "if you will listen—"

"You two join hands and walk down the road!" the girl interrupted.

Rush took the fat man's hand, little-kid fashion. They walked. The fat man's hand was soft, sweating meat. The road was two tracks through the weeds, and when it turned and went behind some trees, there stood a gray roadster with the top down. The roadster was typically Hollywood.

"Rumble seat," the girl said. "Open it."

Rush opened the rumble.

"Get in it," the girl ordered. "Icky is going to lock you both in while she drives."

Rush said, "If you—"

"When you started monkeying with Icky," the girl said belligerently, "you bit off something. She's been watching that Continental Detective Agency all day in hopes of taking one or more of you home with her. When she saw the hearse-load of you pull out, she said to herself, 'Icky, there's a chance. Just follow them and take charge of one or more.' So she did, and here we all are."

Rush said, "You got me wrong. I'm no Continental detective—"

"I don't think so, either, considering the way you were roughing them around."

"Then—"

"Then you're probably one of the guys they want to hang for murdering the *Pacific Queen's* purser," Icky said. "Get in the rumble seat."

THE FAT hearse driver had no consideration. He was big, and at best there was not too much room inside the rumble seat with the lid locked; but if the man had shown consideration and kept himself bunched, it would not have been so bad. It would have been bad—dust kept swirling around and choking them, and Icky seemed to pick her road for the bumps—but it would not have been too bad.

Rush hated to be crowded, and confused, too. And he was several varieties of confused.

The *Pacific Queen*—that was the name she'd mentioned, wasn't it? The *Pacific Queen* was that liner which had run on an island reef off the Mexican coast two months ago. Big stuff for the newspapers. Some of the survivors had supposedly brought ashore a few cases of grog, staged a drunk and a mutiny, and scared the other passengers half out of their wits. It was very stinko business. Among the drowned had been the purser.

The point, Rush recalled, was that the *Pacific Queen* purser's drowned body had been washed up on the island. There had been no murder rumors in the newspapers.

The car drummed along, hit bumps with dependable rapidity. The fat man kept groaning, swearing, and crowding Rush; and Rush kept pinching him and the man would snarl.

Rush said, "Well, well, I should have thought of something before."

He took hold of the fat man's throat, and they had a fight which consisted of grunting, straining and bumping themselves against their surroundings. When Rush had the other man's face a satisfactory shade of purple, he let the fellow get a little air down his throat.

"You—you devil!" the man croaked.

"Talk always calms me down," Rush explained.

"All right, damn you," the man said. "Here is what my brother told me. My brother said—"

"You mean your head-man detective brother?"

"Sure. He said you were Clickell Rush, who had a reputation, and you might gum the works if you weren't put
out of the way. He suggested we grab you and stick you in
a cistern out in the country. He said we wouldn't have had
to worry about you, only you work for some nutty party
named Bufa—"

"Objection!"

"Huh?"

"I don't work for Bufa. I've quit. My new aim in life is
to find this Bufa, whoever he is, and knock his ears loose.
Knock her ears loose, in case it's a her. That's beside the
point. Proceed."

"That's all of it."

"No more about Bufa?"

"Well," the fat man continued, "my brother has been
gettin' a hundred dollars for every unusual crime he could
dig up and telephone to this Bufa. When these sailors first
came to my brother's detective agency with their queer
story, he passed it on to Bufa. That was before my brother
realized what a big thing it was."

"Big?"

The man became silent.

"You aren't thinking of stopping talking?" Rush asked.

"That's all my brother told me," the man said stubbornly.

"By weaseling you on information," Rush said, "your
brother is going to be the cause of you getting a good
choking."

Rush took the man's throat again, set himself to do
squeezing, and while he was doing it, realized the car had
made some sharp turns and stopped.

The car stood motionless. There was stillness and strain
inside the rumble. The fat man could not move, could not
get air, and Rush's fingers clamping his throat made tiny
crunching sounds.

"Oh!" the girl's voice said, outside.

Her one word was loud and strange enough that Rush knew something had happened.

Rush stopped choking the fat man and hit the inside of the rumble with his fists, kicked it with his feet.

"*Yeo-o-o-w!*" he yelled. "Help! Murder! Police!"

The rumble lid opened.

IT HAD not seemed dark inside the rumble seat, but it must have been very dark, because the sunlight blinded Rush. He felt something gouging him and could not see exactly what it was—but he had a good idea.

A voice said, "Hey, mates! Here's two of your private dicks."

Rush could see enough to be sure it was a revolver muzzle gouging him. The man with the gun said, "Get out, shamus!"

The man was dark and beamy. He wore a sweater, a sailor cap which had seen whiter days.

Rush climbed out of the rumble seat and looked around and saw that four more men, all of whom looked like sailors, were menacing Icky. One of them held the girl's rifle.

Behind the men and Icky stood a white stucco and glass house of spectacular design. Where the house was not stucco, it was glass, and there was more glass than white stucco. The house was not large, but it was unusual enough that probably no one had ever seen it without experiencing an impulse to walk around and around it and just look.

Beyond the house spread the sapphire blue, wavescratched surface of the Pacific Ocean.

The hearse driver got out of the rumble seat and stood feeling his throat.

The beamy sailor said, "How'd you get stowed in the stern quarters of her car, detectives?"

The hearse driver jabbed both hands at Rush. He yelled, "This guy ain't—"

Rush hit him. Rush was much smaller, much more wiry, and he seemed to jump up to get at the hearse driver's jaw. The driver turned around twice before he spread out on the ground.

"What he started to say," Rush explained, "is that we're not exactly friends any more. You see, the Continental detectives are chiseling. They've started looking out for themselves. They're double-crossing you."

The sailors gaped at him.

"We figured the wind blew that way," the heavy-set sailor muttered.

Rush looked self-righteous. "Me, I've got ethics," he said. "So if you sailor boys need a private detective, I'm a good bet."

"You want to do the job for us?" the beamy sailor asked.

"Sure," Rush said heartily. "On reasonable terms."

The sailors all grinned.

Their leader said, "Well now, that's nice."

Rush grinned back at them and said, "You just give me a new and full account of all details, and your troubles will be over."

"That's awfully nice of you," the beamy sailor said. "You just come in the house, mate, and we'll get you straightened out."

"You just put your problem on my deck," Rush said heartily.

"We've been hoping," the sailor said, "that we could put our problem on somebody's deck."

When they entered the house, it was to walk through rooms that were more utterly modernistic than anything Rush had ever seen. The photographic murals on the walls struck him, particularly. Almost every wall was covered with great photographs, some scenic, some symbolic, some fantastic in their modernism. They were amazingly good photographs.

"Room over here where we can talk," the beamy sailor said.

He opened a door, stood back. There was gloom on the other side of the door, and Rush knew it was a mistake to step through; but unfortunately he did not know that until he was inside—and the door crashed shut behind him. He threw himself backward, not turning, but he was not quick enough.

He was locked in a dark room.

He threw out his hands and felt to learn what kind of room he was in, and his hands touched a bottle, which fell on the floor and broke. Instantly, a strong chemical odor flooded up around him.

"Poison gas!" he thought.

But it wasn't. It was one of the chemicals used to develop photographic negatives, and nothing to get excited about. He felt along the door edge, located a switch, thumbed it; and when lights came on, he got down and examined the broken bottle. Enough of the label still stuck to one of the pieces. Yes, it was photographic chemical, and not so disturbing.

The dead man leaning against the wall at the back was considerably more disturbing.

CHAPTER III

CAPTAIN AND MATE

RUSH HAD BEEN taught in school—he had read it in books, too—that the human being is in all essentials a flexible piece of construction. That is, a man can get used to anything. Personally, Rush doubted that, although it was true that his contact with dead persons had not been extensive—he had done his level best to keep it so. He had seen some violent deaths, and the last one had not been any easier on his stomach than the first one.

He put off taking his second look at the back of the room as long as there was a reasonable excuse.

The place, he saw, was a photographic darkroom, a chamber fixed up for developing work. The place appeared to be as strong as a vault, with the walls of masonry and the door of steel.

He listened. He heard some harsh laughter outside. Then the girl, Icky, cried out once. There was something about the cry that made Rush feel as if half a dozen cold bugs had gone racing down his spine.

He hit the door. It was steel, not thick steel, but firm enough.

Before he did anything else, Rush made himself examine the dead man. The fellow was gaunt and a little past middle age; he wore a dark uniform with brass buttons. On the breast of the uniform was embroidered the words:

PURSER
S.S. PACIFIC QUEEN

The man's skull had been bashed in with a monkey wrench, and the wrench, gore-stained, lay at the body's feet. The man looked, too, as if he had been beaten a long time before he died.

The body sat on a sandy beach, propped against a palm tree; and in the background, rather dim but nevertheless discernible, was a steamship which had crashed on a reef, and was surrounded by great breaking waves. Rush had seen enough of the newspaper accounts about the wrecking of the *Pacific Queen* to recognize the ship on the reef as that vessel.

The dead man was the most realistic, detailed photograph Rush had ever seen. It was enlarged three feet by four, approximately, but it was still so genuine that it seemed the crimson stains from the smashed skull should go on flowing.

"Whoever made that," Rush muttered, "was something with a camera."

He went back to the door, gave attention to the lock, found the keyhole was large. He pulled a button off his vest and shoved it into the keyhole, the button breaking into fragments inside the lock. He took a second button, this one off his shirt, wet it with his tongue and jammed it into the lock with the vest button.

Rush got back as far as the darkroom permitted and waited, arms over his eyes and face.

The explosion was equal to two or three shotguns letting loose simultaneously. There was some flash, a trifling amount of smoke and flying pieces of what was left of the lock.

The two buttons had been molded of a chemical composition which, when crushed together and dampened, became violently self-explosive.

Rush lowered his arms from his face. A number of bottles of photographic chemicals on the darkroom shelves had been broken. A big enlarger had toppled over, and the top had flipped open.

An automatic pistol had fallen out of the enlarger and lay in a pool of photographic chemical. Rush picked it up, then remembered fingerprints, and tried to wipe it off. He probably succeeded in blurring his fingerprints, but he also got photo dope smeared over the weapon. There were two cartridges left in the clip.

He carried the gun, wrapped in his brown handkerchief, but held so he could fire it if necessary, as he shoved open the wrecked door and stepped out of the darkroom.

The ultra-modern house was full of silence.

He walked to the front door, went out—and stopped with a jerk of astonishment.

He held onto the automatic for an instant, then let it drop.

"Damn!" one of the officers said. "I came within a hair of shooting his insides out!"

"Me, too," the other officer said.

THERE SEEMED to be only the two men. They were not police officers. They were, according to their uniforms, ship's officers. But their guns were police type.

One officer wore an insignia that said:

CAPTAIN
PACIFIC QUEEN

The other's insignia said:

FIRST MATE
PACIFIC QUEEN

Rush said, "What makes you fellows act like cops?"

They ignored the question.

The captain said, "Something familiar about him, isn't there, Mister?"

"Yes, sir," answered the first mate. "But I can't place him."

"I don't think he was on the *Pacific Queen* when she piled up," the captain said.

"No, sir."

Rush said, "A fellow named Clickell Rush has had more or less newspaper notoriety from time to time."

"Yes, I read—" The captain stopped, squinted at Rush. "Oh, I see. You're Clickell Rush. The newspaper stories were quite spectacular, as I recall."

Rush said, "Now that we know who we are—" and started to pick up the automatic.

"I wouldn't!" the captain said.

The first mate pushed Rush against the side of the house with the muzzle of his gun, and searched for weapons, then stepped back grimly.

"You see," he said, "we heard a scream and an explosion, and we're rather curious."

The captain pointed in the direction of the reddish tiled roof which was visible over the tops of the trees.

"We live next door, you know," he said. "We have—ah—somewhat more than a neighborly interest in Miss Icky's welfare."

"Who is this Icky?" Rush asked.

"One of the best women photographers in the world," the captain explained. "She does publicity photographs for our steamship line. She is—she happened to be on the *Pacific Queen* when it struck the reef, as you may know."

Rush, exasperated, said, "What I know about this whole thing would go in a gnat's eye, and—"

"Shut up!" the captain growled. "Mister, will you go in the house and see what is wrong."

The first mate entered the house. Rush frowned at the firm way the captain held the revolver pointed at him, then looked around. The girl's roadster was gone, and so were the sailors, the girl and the hearse driver. It was a peaceful seacoast scene, except for the strong odor of photographic chemicals coming out of the house.

Suddenly, the first mate popped out of the door. He had a wild look.

"He killed Joe!" he shouted, and leveled an arm at Rush.

Rush started, said, "What on—"

But they closed in on him, menacing with their guns, and herded him into the house.

"That dead man's only a picture!" Rush said angrily.

But he wasn't. He was a genuine dead man, about sixty years old, who lay on the kitchen floor.

THERE WAS complete confusion in Rush's mind. Nothing stood out of it except that there was a dead man on the kitchen floor. A man who had been shot at least three times, one of the bullets having been fired after the body had fallen—for the first mate had dug the bullet out of the floor.

The first mate rolled the death bullet around in his palm.

"A .45," he said grimly. "Same caliber as the gun he had when he came out of the front door."

Rush looked everywhere but at the body. "Who is he?"

"Joe—Icky's gardener," the captain growled. "What happened? Did Joe catch you searching the house for the picture?"

"Picture?"

"The picture they're after," the captain said savagely. "Don't be dumb."

Rush said, "Let me show you something," and turned, keeping his hands up, and walked to the darkroom. He nodded at the picture of the dead man sitting against the darkroom rear wall.

"You mean that picture?"

The captain said, "Hell, no; of course not! That's evidence my purser was murdered, is all. We'll use it at the trial after we catch whoever killed the purser. But it's not important. My officers, Icky and myself can all swear on the stand that he was murdered."

"Looks as if he was beaten first," Rush said.

"Sure. Tortured."

"Why?"

The two *Pacific Queen* officers were silent. There was a salty draft through the rooms, and the washing of waves against the foot of the cliff on which the house stood was audible. Somewhere in the near-by trees a bird was singing joyfully.

The captain had been thinking over something, and now he got it off his chest.

"American ships are the most seaworthy ships in the world," he said. "And American officers and sailors are as fine a class as you'll find on any of the oceans. I say that, and I'll stand behind it in spite of any publicity, some of which I suspect is not at all displeasing to alien shipping interests, to the contrary. The *Pacific Queen* went on that reef in a gale, and it was unavoidable. Every passenger was saved—and that was due to the utmost heroism on the part of my crew, and don't think it wasn't— Now, in that crew, there were a few bad men. A very few. And they were very bad. It was those men who murdered the poor purser because—well, I'm not going to have the mess plastered in the newspapers until we have the truth. So this is all I'm saying."

Rush said, "Let me get this straight. Icky has a picture, and some sailors want it?"

"Some sailors," the captain admitted sourly. "You may be working with them."

"The sailors hired private detectives to help them get the picture, evidently," Rush said. "And the detectives thought the picture important enough that they tried to grab it themselves, and to the devil with the sailors."

"We didn't know—"

"I'm the guy," Rush said, "that nobody seems to want around."

"You—"

"What is the picture?" Rush demanded.

They shook their heads stubbornly.

"In that case," Rush said, "it's everybody for himself, kinda."

He was standing in half an inch of photographic chemical—the door had been equipped with a threshold to make it lightproof, and this low dam kept the chemicals in the room.

"This stuff"—Rush pointed at the chemical pool—"may put our eyes out if we get too much of it."

He let this exaggeration soak in.

Then he swiped a foot sidewise through the chemical, knocked the stuff sheeting up over the two officers. They dodged wildly, shielding their eyes.

Rush left.

CHAPTER IV

PICTURE TRAIL

GOING THROUGH THE darkroom door, Rush made a pass at it, knocked it shut. He went on across a living room, through another door—this was a swinging door, which had no lock—and into the kitchen, where he veered right to snatch a box marked "Pepper" off a cabinet. He tore the box apart in the middle, flung the pepper flakes up into the kitchen air, left the powdery stuff swirling there, and went on outdoors, banging the door shut behind him, all without more than perceptibly slackening his speed.

The lawn was a cropped modernistic thing—no hedges, no shrubbery. He glued elbows to his ribs, went into sprint stride until he reached brush, low trees and rocks on the seaward aide of the house. Once under cover, he changed speed for caution.

He saw the two officers come out of the house. They had gone through the pepper. They rubbed their eyes, sneezed and swore.

Rush crept through the brush. A thought having hit him, he turned left and worked toward the house at which the captain had pointed when he said, "We live next door, you know." Reaching more open woodland which was hidden from Icky's modernistic house, Rush ran again, galloped up boldly to the other house.

This one was not at all like Icky's house, being of the old-English country home style, small and rather attractive in a pleasantly homelike way. Rush walked to the front door and glanced through the screen.

He saw a tastefully furnished parlor. A bright Navajo Indian blanket was spread on the floor, and on this lay a baby. The baby looked at Rush, cooed and waved its hands.

Rush punched the doorbell.

Shortly a woman came to the door, a pleasant, attractive and capable-looking woman.

"May I use your telephone?" Rush asked. "I presume you are the captain's wife?"

The woman seemed puzzled.

"My husband," she said, "is a real-estate man downtown."

Rush straightened his brown necktie thoughtfully.

"Look," he said, "do you have the captain and first mate of a passenger liner staying here?"

The woman shook her head. "No. Only my husband, myself and the baby live here."

Rush put his hands in his pockets and considered.

"In that case, I guess I won't make that telephone call," he said.

He turned away.

"Just a minute," the woman said.

"Eh?" Rush stopped.

"Is Icky Benson in trouble? I thought I heard some noises over there a few minutes ago, but I was in the bathroom washing the baby's things, and couldn't be sure."

"What makes you ask that?" Rush inquired. "I didn't mention Icky."

The woman eyed him.

"Yes, but Icky said something to me a few days ago about a captain and a first mate of the *Pacific Queen*," the housewife explained. "Icky said that if I saw the captain or first mate prowling around, I was to call her. She said they meant her no good."

Rush said, "Icky was afraid of them?"

"Yes."

"And they don't live here?"

"No."

"I'm obfuscated."

"Eh?"

"Confused," Rush explained.

He walked away rubbing his jaw thoughtfully.

WHEN HE was concealed in the brush again, he stopped and gave the little English-style home a long, thoughtful examination; after that there was no doubt in his mind but that this was the house which the captain had meant when he pointed and said, "We live next door, you know." This was the only next-door house; there wasn't another house within eye range.

It was hard to think that the captain had been anything but a liar.

Rush went back toward Icky's house. He did it cautiously, then lay behind a bush and watched the house for a long time without seeing any sign of life.

Then he heard a man sneeze over among the trees to the south. He crept in that direction, and located the captain and the first mate standing behind trees and watching Icky's house. The two mariners were holding their guns in a way that indicated they were eager to shoot somebody.

Their trees stood a little distance apart, so they had to lift their voices to speak to each other; and that, with the direction of the wind, enabled Rush to overhear some of what they said.

"We should've shot him right off the bat!" the first mate grumbled.

"Don't complain, Mister," snapped the captain. "We had to frame all the murders onto somebody."

"All the murders?"

"Yes, Mister," the captain said. "The law has got to have somebody they can prove murdered the purser and Joe. Also Icky Benson and as many of those damned private detectives as we have to get rid of."

"But this Rush wasn't on the *Pacific Queen,* so he couldn't have killed the purser," the first mate objected.

"I can change the passenger list," the captain growled. "Give me a pen and ink and the passenger list, and he can't prove he didn't sail. Not when half a dozen of us swear he did." The captain laughed harshly. "Why, hell, I rescued him off the liner personally. Don't you remember?"

The first mate chuckled. "Aye, aye, sir," he said. "I remember."

"Then let's get the devil out of here," the captain said.

Rush had a bad ten minutes when he thought they might have a car concealed in the neighborhood, in which case he would have to do something drastic, because he didn't have a way of following a car. But they kept walking, striding along briskly, their guns shoved out of sight in waistbands.

The day was going. The sun stood low on the horizon, with clouds partly in front of it, and long fan-shaped beams of sunlight were shoving through rifts in the clouds. The sea had darkened, and now and then a wave broke in a long white ghost of foam which quickly faded. The air was pleasantly cool and had a tang of brine.

The captain and the mate went down the cliff and got on a boat.

RUSH FOUND the sea to be cold. He was no lover of cold water, and after he was in it, he took time out to give way to a thorough shake. He stood behind a huge boulder, being knocked around by the waves, hating the cold water, and hating practically everything else that he could think of.

"Blast that Bufa!" he gritted.

He thought of a number of unholy things he hoped to do to Bufa, the voice of the wired-wireless toad, if he ever caught the individual; and that warmed him up somewhat.

Swimming was something he did well, even when it was necessary to do most of it underwater. He came down on the boat from out of the sun, reasoning that men on boats do not stand around looking into the sun. The waves were breaking high, and that helped hide him, but did not help swimming.

The boat had a rusty chain bobstay that ran from the bow water line up to a swordfishing pulpit mounted on a wide, stubby bowsprit. Rush swung up on the bobstay, sat there, and let his clothes leak their water.

Fifty feet would catch the length of the boat, and about fifteen feet its beam. That was wide. It was a squat old hooker which needed paint, varnish and brass polish. An ancient steam yacht which had gone down the nautical grade until it was evidently a party fishing boat. All-day fishing, tackle, your lunch—two dollars.

Rush climbed on deck.

He took a good look first, saw no one in sight, then swung over the iron pipe rail. He sat down at once and took off his shoes, then carried them in his hands, sidled down the deck and went into the first companionway he came to. He found himself in a forecastle, with a pile of anchor rope behind him and plenty of old boat smells in the air.

In front of him was a bulkhead and an open door. Through the door, voices.

Icky was saying, "That is the picture, and that is the spot—right where the purser is standing. Right under his feet."

She sounded like a very terrified girl.

CHAPTER V

TROUBLE AND ROCKS

THE CAPTAIN'S VOICE said, "Do you believe her, Mister?"

"No, sir," said the first mate. "Not entirely, sir."

The beamy sailor's voice said, "Mates, she may be dealin' it to a straight, an' she may not."

The hearse driver said, "If you guys don't turn me loose, you're gonna wish you had! When my brother, the private detective, finds out—"

There was a blow. The hearse driver croaked in agony.

"And you'll stay shut up," the captain ordered.

Icky said wildly, "I tell you, that's the picture."

"We're not convinced," the captain said. "Boys, work on her some more."

There was scuffling, moaning from the girl, and Rush got ready to step through the bulkhead door—but didn't, because they let the girl talk.

"I was with the purser the whole time," Icky said desperately. "He was an old friend of my father's. You know that."

"Sure," the captain said. "We know—"

"The purser told me he knew you and some of the others were after the contents of the ship's safe. He'd overheard you. He wanted me to help him, and I did. We got the passengers' jewels and the money out of the safe. There was a half-million-dollars' worth, at least. We put it in two big suitcases, and got ashore in one of the lifeboats with

116

the passengers. We buried both suitcases at once. It was daylight. The purser wanted a record of where we buried the suitcases. That picture there shows the purser standing over the place where the suitcases, containing half a million from the *Pacific Queen's* safe, are buried."

"You're sure of that?" the captain demanded.

"Just as sure as I am that you went into a blind rage when you learned what the purser had done, and killed him because you couldn't torture the hiding place out of him."

The girl's voice lifted as she continued.

"And the purser moaned something about pictures when he was dying!" she screamed. "So you knew that I had a photographic record of the hiding place. I could tell that. I knew you were trying to corner me. I hid from you and your man. You couldn't find me. When you got ashore, you hired detectives to try and locate me—"

"We sure did," snarled the hearse driver. "He hired my brother—"

There was another blow, another squawk of agony, and no more out of the hearse driver.

The captain's voice said, "Do you believe her now, Mister?"

"A little, sir," said the first mate.

"We've got to be convinced," the captain said. "Boys, work on her some more. If that water is boiling now, pour some of it in her eyes."

That brought Rush into the cabin.

RUSH ENTERED in a hurry, because it seemed like a time to hurry. He threw a shoe. It hit the face of one sailor who was holding a kettle of boiling water, and he squawked, threw up his arms, and boiling water sheeted over two other sailors, which did no harm.

In the cabin were six sailors, captain, first mate, hearse driver, and Icky. The latter two were tied hand and foot. All guns were in pockets or holsters.

The captain was holding a photograph the size of a sheet of typewriting paper.

One sailor was now slightly stunned, and two a trifle scalded.

Rush had one shoe left. He did his best to brain the captain with it, missed, and the shoe flew through a porthole and he never saw it again.

Rush made no effort to stay in the cabin. In seconds, he figured, they would begin shooting bullets into him. So he kept going straight for the rear, did what damage he could en route.

He horned a man violently with his doubled elbow. The fellow yelped. He would do more than yelp in a few moments, because there was a hypodermic device molded in sponge rubber and adhering to Rush's elbow. A blow with the elbow would put enough chemical in a man to stupefy him completely in a remarkably short time.

Rush kept going. He grabbed a life preserver, and sloughed the first mate with it, knocking the man backward into another sailor. Rush held onto the life preserver.

Rush scooped up Icky, still keeping the life preserver. He kept going. Somehow, in passing the galley, he collected a butcher knife. Out on deck, he plunged.

He had stormed the length of the cabin in not much more than ten seconds.

He slashed, got the girl's wrist ropes apart. He jammed the life preserver in her hands.

"Under stern!" he hissed.

He shoved her overboard.

He went down, doubling, tearing at his necktie. He got it off, wadded it, and jammed it into the "Charlie Noble"—

the name sailors applied, no telling why, to the stovepipe which comes up through the deck. The stovepipe was hot and smoking; for they'd had a fire to heat the boiling water.

Toward the bows, Rush went. He still had the butcher knife. He shot forward, stomach-down, and slid the last dozen feet. Not because he wanted to be spectacular, or liked splinters, but because the men were out of the cabin now, and had started shooting.

He chopped with the butcher knife, got the anchor rope apart.

"Help!" the hearse driver was bellowing. "Get me away from 'em!" The waves began tossing the boat toward the rock-fanged shore.

Rush slid down the forecastle hatch, back into the boat. All the men were out on deck, swearing and running.

"He dived overboard!" a man yelled. "I heard the splash."

Not wanting them to look overside and find the girl, Rush dived forward into the cabin. He swooped on the hearse driver, the butcher knife held ready to cut the man loose.

The hearse driver misunderstood the purpose of the poised butcher knife.

His scream of terror must have been heard in Los Angeles.

UP ON deck, the men boiled back toward the cabin companion. Rush sawed at the hearse driver's ropes with the butcher knife. It seemed to him that the butcher knife was the dullest thing he had ever handled. But he got the hearse driver free.

"Gosh!" The driver started to get up, croaked, "I thought—"

Rush shoved him back.

"*Ps–s–t!*" Rush said. "Take 'em by surprise."

Rush then jumped for a dark hole. He landed below, in the engine room. Tools stuck in mountings on the wall, and he began picking out hammers and wrenches, the heavier ones, for ammunition.

Just then, the necktie let loose in the stove. It made a sound that might have been a firecracker which had fizzled.

The necktie was supposed to do better than that. The lining was saturated with a combination of explosive and one of the chemical materials designated under the common heading of tear gas. But then, the necktie was wet.

Men were down in the cabin now. Rush threw a hammer. He threw it at a man's head. The hammer was heavy, and he couldn't tell how hard to throw it and merely stun, so he took no chances and threw hard enough to remove doubt. The victim dropped.

The hearse driver reached, got himself a leg, and went into action.

Rush missed with two wrenches. He hated that, because they were his two biggest wrenches. Then two men began shooting down into the engine room at him, and he got behind the engine.

The boat hit the rocks. She lifted high, and seemed to jump onto the rock. The crash was terrific. Then the boat rolled over on her side.

Rush lunged to the companion. Sure enough, the two who had been shooting at him were down on the floor. The striking of the boat had upset them. They scrambled around. The gas from the stove was making them cry.

Reaching up, Rush tapped one's skull with a wrench. Then he hit the other in the face, throwing the wrench. He followed up, landed a fist on the fellow's jaw.

The hearse driver got his foe by the ears about then, and hammered the man's head on a bulkhead until he was limp.

"Out!" Rush yelled. "That gas!"

His own eyes began smarting. But they did not smart enough to prevent him finding the captain, and taking the picture which was the cause of everything.

Out on deck, the air was clear. But the waves were lifting the boat and slamming it onto the rocks. The craft was close in now—in fact, the bow was jammed high on the beach.

"Icky—you all right?" Rush yelled.

Icky came out from behind a big boulder on shore.

"Save that picture!" she screamed.

Rush dashed into the cabin, got a sailor by the collar, dragged him to the bow, hit him with a monkey wrench to insure his remaining unconscious, and threw him off on shore.

He repeated the carry-out-knock-senseless-throw-ashore procedure until he had unloaded the old boat.

The hearse driver fell off the bow onto the beach without assistance.

"Now," Rush said, "we call the police."

"We call my brother," the hearse driver said.

"No," Rush said. "We call the police—"

The hearse driver drew a big revolver which he must have taken off one of the sailors.

"We call my brother!" he said.

CHAPTER VI
TOAD EGG

CLICKELL RUSH WAS—HE still thought so—more of an inventor than a detective. As an inventor, he had imagination. The two things held hands, as it were, for it was necessary to have imagination to be an inventor.

Imagination or no imagination, Rush considered the saga of himself and Bufa—the toad with the wired-wireless voice—to be nothing if not fantastic. If anybody had told him the story offhand, he knew very well he would not have believed it.

So he hated to tell the story. But sometimes he had to tell it, and when he did, he always finished warm under the collar, and saying, "Now don't start telling me how whacky it sounds!"

At nine o'clock that night, he was looking around hotly and saying, "Now don't start telling me how whacky it sounds!"

The head-man private detective, and his brother the hearse driver, nodded solemnly.

A dozen or more other private detectives, and some policemen also nodded profoundly.

Rush was astounded.

"You believe me!" he said weakly.

The head-man private detective nodded. "Sure. I been getting one hundred dollars for every unusual crime I could notify this Bufa about. I don't know who Bufa is, or anything, except I found a crate of carrier pigeons on my lawn one day, and orders to tie notes about unusual crimes to a bird's leg and turn it loose. I did that. Every time the crime was good, I'd get a hundred-dollar bill."

Rush said, "I don't wish any man bad luck, but I hope you never make any more of that money."

All the private detectives grinned.

"The hell with Bufa," the head man said. "We're set. When them sailors came to me with the story about the picture, and wanted me to find the girl and get the picture, I unluckily first notified Bufa, then got to thinking, and knew the sailors were crooks. I went to the steamship company, and they said if I would trap the sailors and get the goods on 'em, I would get all the steamship company business. And boy, that steamship company business is a plum."

The head man got up, scowled at Rush, said, "I didn't want you solving it and glomming the gravy. I was sure sorry I notified Bufa for a measly hundred bucks. So all we could do was grab you, and keep you off the job until we did our stuff. And by the way, we didn't exactly mean that about breaking your legs. We was kinda buildin' up a scare to keep you in that cistern until we trapped the sailors. Just forget it, see?"

"I won't forget it!" Rush yelled angrily. "I've got a notion to take a chair to the whole crowd—"

"Pipe down!" a policeman ordered.

Icky got up and said angrily, "Detective, why didn't you tell me this in the first place?"

The head-man detective snorted. "You didn't turn the picture over to the steamship line. I figured you a crook."

"Crook!" Icky shrieked irately. "Those sailors watched the steamship line's offices! I was even afraid they had the telephones tapped!"

"Don't yell at me!" the detective said.

"I'll yell all—"

"Pipe down, lady," another policeman said.

Rush said, "We're orphans, Icky. Nobody loves us."

"Ain't that the truth!" Icky snapped. "A bunch of blood-thirsty sailors chase me, murder my gardener, kidnap me—"

"They're in jail, ain't they?" the policeman interrupted. "Pipe down, lady."

"Orphans is right!" Icky said.

"Let's blow," Rush suggested.

They blew.

THEY RODE a taxicab up the street that led from the police station, and when they had covered half a dozen blocks, Rush remembered something, unbuttoned his shirt.

He took out the picture, which had been tucked inside his shirt.

"Look what I forgot," he said.

They looked at the picture. It was a photograph of an island shore, some rocks, a few trees, the *Pacific Queen* on a reef in the background, and the purser of the ship standing in the foreground.

"Treasure map," Rush said.

"Yeah," Icky said. "I guess we better turn it over to the steamship company, so they'll know where to dig for the contents of the *Pacific Queen's* safe."

Rush nodded. "That straightens everything out. Captain, first mate and sailors were crooks. Private detectives were honest, but glory-hogging. That leaves the two innocent bystanders—you and me."

Icky eyed him. "You sound," she said, "as if you were leading up to something."

Rush grinned. "Dinner for the innocent bystanders. How about it?"

"Swell," Icky said.

Rush thought it was swell, too, and began to believe California might not be so bad.

He was thinking how swell California might be when he walked into his hotel room—he had come to dress for the evening—and saw the toad sitting on the table. It was about a suitcase full of toad, river-mud-yellow underneath, a bad shade of green on top, with warts. It sat with the lighted table lamp close to its gaping mouth. An electric-light cord leading from it was plugged into a wall socket.

Bufa, the toad, was back.

Rush ran over, lifted the toad, looked under it. Sure enough, there was a bank note underneath—a bank note for ten thousand dollars. The ten thousand was Bufa's accustomed payment when Rush had solved a case.

Rush found it hard to eye ten thousand dollars, and still look mad.

"Oh, boy—aren't we happy to see each other!" the toad said unexpectedly.

Rush strode to the window and looked out and saw thousands of lighted windows of Los Angeles spread before him. From any one of many of them, the voice of Bufa the toad might have been watching with binoculars.

THE WILD INDIANS

NO ONE WOULD BELIEVE THAT
THE GADGET MAN WAS INVOLVED
IN A MESS BECAUSE THERE WAS
A TOAD THAT TALKED!

CHAPTER I

HEAP HURRY

HE WAS AN Indian, a rather lean and wiry American Indian, and he had three feathers in his hair—two red feathers and a yellow one. He scraped the feathers against the top of the cabin door when he got into the plane, and one feather fell out and was caught by the wind from the propellers and blown away. The Indian got out of the plane and chased the feather, his blanket flying, his moccasined feet making *sput, sput, sput* sounds as he ran. The Indian caught the feather, returned it to his hair, gathered his blanket about himself with dignity, and walked back to the plane and got in.

"Ugh!" he said.

Sitting in the plane seat, he could see the reflection of his deep-copper features in the plane window. He studied this reflection.

He decided he looked enough like a genuine Indian to fool anybody.

"Ugh!" he said with deep approval. *"Ugh!"*

The newspaper reporter from Tulsa, who stood in front of the airport office, lowered his camera. He had been pointing the camera at the Indian, and now he grinned at the bystanders and winked.

"Nice candid shot," he said.

The bystanders grinned back at him as people, for some reason or other, always seem to grin at somebody they think might put their picture in the newspapers.

The reporter was stubby and dressed the sloppy way that the movies have led the public to expect. A card in his hatband said, *"PRESS."* Also carefully penciled in heavy writing on the card were the words, *"TULSA GLOBE."*

The reporter went to the plane with his camera and climbed in. He took a seat across the aisle from the Indian.

The Indian leaned over and held a cupped palm under the reporter's nose.

"Ugh!" the Indian requested. "Four bits."

"Huh?"

"Ugh! Four bits."

The reporter looked astounded. "Say, Hiawatha, what the hell—"

The Indian kept his cupped palm under the reporter's nose.

"You take picture. Four bits."

"Now listen, chief—"

"No chief. Me plain brave." The Indian held his cupped palm patiently. "Four bits regular price to let paleface take picture. Cough up. *Ugh!*"

The reporter shook his head.

"Be reasonable, Sitting Bull. I'm a newspaper reporter. Me put heap big picture in heap big newspaper, savvy? Heap good thing. *Ugh.*"

"Four bits," the Indian said, "in heap hurry."

"The hell with you, Pocahontas!"

The Indian turned his cupped hand over, dropped it; the hand fell on the reporter's camera and the reporter grabbed for the camera, but he was too late to keep the Indian from getting it.

"Ugh!" the Indian said. "Now me take picture."

He lifted the camera, put the finder to his eye, pointed it at the reporter, and his forefinger poised over the shutter release.

The reporter came up out of his seat screaming in terror. **IT WAS** a pleasant June afternoon, the sun shining bright and hot on this Oklahoma City airport, and breeze, coming in from the oil wells that had almost taken over the city, brought an odor of crude oil; while in the distance could be seen the taller buildings of the midtown business district, standing bright and neat in the sunlight.

The plane doors had been closed, the motors had started drumming, and the plane was taxiing slowly along the ground, chased by a large animated worm of brown dust.

The reporter finished his terrified scream, eyes still fixed on the camera. By now, he was out of his seat. He lunged down the aisle toward the cabin door in terror-stricken flight.

The stewardess tried to get in his way, but he elbowed her clear. Then he tore open the door, jumped out of the moving plane, and since he did not take time to use the proper technique in alighting from a moving object, he fell to the ground and became a rolling bundle of arms and legs. He got up and ran.

Behind him, in the plane, the Indian was in pursuit. But he had become entangled with his blanket, and lost time. He finally got lined out and dashed down the aisle, holding the blanket clear of his legs with one hand, carrying the camera with the other hand. He bounded out of the plane, did not fall, and took up the chase.

Indian and newspaper reporter went across the airport. The reporter lost ground, but he was still ahead when he doubled through a gate into a fenced enclosure provided for the parking of spectators' cars.

The reporter sprang into a long, expensive roadster. This car had started moving shortly after the reporter sprang out of the plane. It was driven by a man who had wide shoulders, who wore an extraordinary amount of fawn-colored cowboy hat, and who had a bright bandanna handkerchief knotted around his neck. The man had pulled the handkerchief up and it now hid that part of his face below his eyes.

Roadster, reporter and the man who was hiding his face all left in haste.

The Indian, having lost the race, came to a stop. He threw back his head and emitted a lengthy and rather elaborate war whoop, modulating it in the approved fashion by patting his mouth with his hand.

The plane had stopped. The Indian arranged his blanket and walked back with dignity, carrying the camera out at shoulder height in front of him, as though it were a scalp.

The plane pilot, co-pilot and stewardess all had questions to ask him.

"*Ugh!*" the Indian explained. "Reporter paleface a hyperphotophobiac."

"A what?"

"*Ugh.*"

There did not seem to be much more that could be done about the peculiar incident, because the Indian now reduced his vocabulary to a series of *"Ughs."* So the big passenger plane took off and flew to Tulsa.

TULSA FROM the air had a more clustered appearance than Oklahoma City, particularly the business district, where the tall skyscrapers that oil had built were grouped closely and, from a distance, gave the appearance of being minarets on a medieval castle.

The plane came in across Mohawk Park and the reservoir, landed at the municipal airport and taxied up to the big hangars that stood across the road from the flying school.

The co-pilot sprang out of the plane and disappeared inside the waiting room.

Porters began unloading baggage from the plane. Over half of the total baggage consisted of dark saddle-leather cases, all with the same color, workmanship, handles and hardware, but of different sizes and shapes. These similar cases were placed in a separate stack.

The Indian found a taxicab, and was helping the driver load the stack of similar bags into the cab when the co-pilot came out of the waiting room and approached.

"Well, I found a dictionary," the co-pilot said.

The Indian did not seem interested.

"Hyperphotophobia," the co-pilot said, "is being scared of a camera, eh?"

"Ugh," the Indian agreed. "Special kind of scared."

The taxicab hauled the Indian into Tulsa, where he registered at the most impressive hotel, and gave the bellboy who carried the bags a five-dollar tip.

"Ps-s-s-t!" the bellboy told his fellows. "Rich Osage Indian in Suite 1103."

The word went around.

The Indian, left alone in his hotel room, took the camera to the window. He opened the window.

Across the street stood a building topped by a flagpole from which flew a flag advertising used cars; and behind this was another, higher building, the side of which was a solid blank wall of brick.

The Indian aimed the camera at the flag which advertised used cars. He peered into the view-finder, which was a telescopic thing with lenses and crossed wires.

He pressed the shutter trip. Something went *clank!* inside the camera. The rope holding the flag came apart. The flag fluttered down. Beyond, a puff of brick dust flew out of the wall.

"*Ugh!*" the Indian said. "Telescopic sight and everything."

He sat down on the bed, took a screwdriver out of one of the similar cases, and dismantled the camera.

The silenced single-shot pistol inside the camera did not shoot through the lens. Nothing so crude as that. There was a mechanical arrangement which whisked the lens aside the instant the shot was fired.

CHAPTER II

THE GADGET MAN

THE TOAD WAS about the size of a medium-built bulldog, and it had some of the characteristics of a bulldog, particularly an, "I'd-as-soon-eat-your-leg-off-as-not!" expression around the eyes. The toad was made cleverly of papier-mâché and other material molded over a brass framework, and it had a mossy-looking back with warts, a belly the color of the Missouri River. It sat with its red mouth perpetually wide open.

The Indian got this toad out of one of the cases, plugged a connecting wire into a wall socket.

He took the shade off the electric table light, switched the light on and maneuvered the glowing bulb inside the toad's mouth; then he waited.

Soon the heat from the bulb caused a thermostat concealed under the toad's tongue to close; this switched on a wired-radio "transceiver" also hidden in the toad, and the Indian was now ready to hold a conversation with someone hooked on to the city-lighting system with another "transceiver."

He leaned close to the toad's ear, where the microphone was concealed.

"Do you know how many times I've been called Hiawatha since I left Los Angeles?" he demanded sourly.

The voice of the toad chuckled. This time, the voice sounded as though it were being disguised by speaking through about two feet of rubber hose.

"And that is all that happened to you—being called Hiawatha?" the voice asked.

"All that happened until I got to Oklahoma City," the Indian said sourly.

"And in Oklahoma City?"

"The newspaper reporter came around."

"Newspaper reporter?"

"He said so. He wasn't a very good actor, and I got the idea right away that he had come out to the airport looking for me."

"For Johnny One Arrow, you mean," the voice of the toad suggested.

"O.K. The reporter asked the plane pilot to be sure, and the pilot said I was Johnny One Arrow. So the reporter pointed his camera at me and waited for a good ripe time to shoot me, only in this case the shooting was to be done with a silenced pistol of a thing inside the camera."

The Indian had been speaking in a perfectly clear, normal and rather grim voice, which bore no trace of an aboriginal accent, and he did not resort to any more *"Ughs!"*

"Just as I got in the plane," he continued, "the reporter drew his bead, so I had to knock a feather out of my hair and keep very busy chasing it. You see, a target has to stand still before you can get a sure-fire sight on it with the camera thing."

"Then what?" the toad asked.

"Then the reporter got away." The Indian leaned closer to the toad, and wearing a dark scowl, but speaking in a pleasant voice, asked, "You wouldn't be going to surprise me?"

"Surprise you?"

"You wouldn't," the Indian said, "be going to tell me what it is all about?"

The toad chuckled long and gleefully.

"And spoil the fun?" it asked.

"One of these times it's gonna be me who gets spoiled," the Indian said, and glared.

"You got one half of a ten-thousand-dollar bill, didn't you?"

"I know, but—"

"And you've always gotten the other half of the bill when you solved a case, haven't you?"

The Indian lost his temper and began yelling.

"Blast it!" he shouted. "Who tried to kill me in Oklahoma City?"

"A newspaper reporter, you said."

"Why, I mean?"

"Because you were pretending to be Johnny One Arrow."

The toad seemed to be enjoying itself.

"They didn't know," it added, *"that you were Clickell Rush."*

The toad chuckled some more.

"Now that you've got the bear by the tail," it said, *"let's see you find the bear."*

CLICKELL RUSH took the black-haired wig containing the three feathers off his head, threw it on the floor, stamped on it; then, he took off his brightly colored blanket, wadded it and hurled it at the bed, but the blanket spread out in the air and landed on the bed with a gentleness which in no way expressed the thrower's wrath.

He jammed his face close to the ugly face of the toad.

"I quit!" he howled. "I won't mess with another one of these crazy cases! I quit! I'm done! If it's the last thing I ever—"

He stopped, because the toad was silent; the other "transceiver" had been switched off.

Rush sat down on the bed, fists jammed on his knees, and eyed the toad—Bufa. That was the name the voice sometimes gave the thing. *"Bufa, of the species* Bufonidæ, *which feeds upon slugs and snails—human variety."* That was what the voice sometimes said.

"Nutty!" Rush said. "Nutty as a squirrel's idea of Heaven."

It had all started months ago when Click Rush, inventor of almost a thousand gadgets for catching crooks, had gone to New York hoping to peddle his inventions to police departments, and had been laughed at as a crank.

He came away beaten.

Then he found Bufa, the toad, in his hotel room, complete with instructions as to how to make it talk.

Rush was to turn detective and use his inventions to solve an unusual crime, after which he'd get the other half of a ten-thousand-dollar bill on which the gadget man had found the toad was sitting. That was what the toad had said. It was fantastic. But he had solved that crime, and now—

Well, he was still solving fantastic crimes. But now he didn't want to, and probably that was the most zany part of the whole mad business—he hadn't been able to stop being a gadget detective. The unknown voice of the toad, Bufa, was managing to involve him in weird crimes, against his will. He was being outsmarted. For months now, Bufa had been too slick for him.

Bufa was clever. Bufa must be wealthy. Bufa might be man or woman and Bufa enjoyed watching Rush solve fantastic mysteries enough to pay ten thousand dollars per show. Whether Bufa actually watched Rush work, or only read about it in the newspapers, still was a mystery.

To stop being a gadget detective, it seemed Rush would have to learn the identity of Bufa.

As for this present business—in Los Angeles, Rush had found half of a ten-thousand-dollar bill in his hotel room, and the voice of the toad had told him to disguise himself as an Indian, call himself "Johnny One Arrow," and fly to Tulsa. That was all.

Rush tried to tell himself he was not following instructions because of the ten thousand dollars involved; it was to get a line on Bufa's identity.

Confusion seemed to be all he had gotten so far.

RUSH REPLACED the dark-haired, three-feathered Indian wig on his head, then retrieved the blanket and wrapped it around his shoulders.

He walked to the closet door, which had a full-length mirror, and examined his reflection in the mirror, changing the drape of the blanket, trying various stances, making assorted faces at himself.

"*Ugh!*" he said disapprovingly. "Sometimes I wonder if you ain't heap crazy and imagining all this stuff."

The telephone interrupted with a quarrelsome snarl.

"Hotel porter speaking," a voice said. "Shall we send your trunk up?"

"Trunk?" Rush said quizzically.

"Yes. It just arrived."

"Where from?"

There was a delay, evidently while the porter examined labels on the trunk. "From Los Angeles."

Rush absent-mindedly scratched his head, and one of the feathers fell out.' He picked up the feather and contemplated it sourly.

"Send it up," he told the porter.

After he pronged the telephone receiver, he carefully stuck the feather back in his black wig.

He had not shipped any trunk from Los Angeles.

He sat there, pondered this development, told himself the sensible thing to do was quit it now, until knuckles drummed the door.

"Come in," Rush said, supposing it was the porter with the trunk.

Three Indians came in. They did not wear blankets or feathers, were very modern-looking Indians, and the most modern part of them was the automatic pistols they presented for inspection as soon as they were inside the door.

They seemed in no hurry. They gave him plenty of time to inspect the gun snouts.

They were young Indians; under thirty, Rush judged, although it was hard to tell. Their suits appeared to be tailored, their shoes had been shined recently and their clothing was all in good taste, although the neckties were a little loud.

Finally, one said, "Where is Johnny One Arrow?"

"Me Johnny One Arrow," Rush replied with dignity.

"Who you kidding?"

"Eh?"

"Johnny One Arrow," the Indian said, "is my father."

"How, papoose," Rush said gravely.

"Where's the trunk?"

Rush said, "It's not the bunk. I wouldn't tell anybody any bunk, because bunking is not my line—"

"Trunk—*trunk!* You heard me!" The Indian shoved his gun forward a foot. "Quit stalling! Where's the trunk?"

Rush shook his head.

"You've got me confused," he complained.

"You're liable to get your system full of lead, if you don't talk fast!" advised the Indian with the gun.

Rush shook his head regretfully.

"Now, papoose, you wouldn't shoot your old pappy, I hope?" he said.

The Indian looked at his two companions.

"He must be crazy."

"Hell, Andy, he's kidding you," one of the others said.

The Indian called Andy put his gun in a pocket. "You keep him covered," he ordered. "I'm going to kick some of his ribs in and see if that helps."

Andy came around to the side of the bed and shoved Rush violently, so that Rush fell from the bed, landed sitting on the floor. Andy said, "Papoose, eh?" He drew back a foot and kicked Rush in the side.

There was a report a little louder than a rotten egg breaking, and Rush and Andy instantly seemed to turn into a cloud of black smoke.

INSIDE THE smoke, Andy began whooping in agony. The smoke was by no means bulletproof, and Rush worked fast. He kept hold of Andy's leg, kept twisting it. Andy continued howling, then fell. Rush slugged with one fist, hitting Andy the first time, but hitting the hard floor with the second blow, and hurting his fist. Then Andy got away.

Rush came erect, dived for the bathroom, got inside, slammed the door, turned the lock and landed in the bathtub. He was an average-size man, and he made himself fit the bottom of the bathtub as closely as possible. He lay there hoping the bathtub was bulletproof.

It wasn't. Three bullets came through the door, hit the tub, and there was a clank and crack of cast iron; after which, the whole side fell out of the tub.

Rush got out of the tub and threw up the bathroom window. Outside, there was a smooth brick wall, with hard cement sidewalk ten floors below. But to the right was the bathroom window of an adjacent room.

More bullets were coming through the door, splintering holes around the lock.

Rush sat in the window. There was a small amount of smoke still coming from under his blanket, and it bothered his eyes. He wrenched off the blanket and let it fall lazily toward the street. Then he tossed away the smoke-bomb gadget which had been under the blanket; the gadget fell, still smoking, and passed the blanket.

Stretching, reaching, gritting his teeth, Rush got one hand on the ledge of the other window. He swung, hanging by the one hand—

He pulled up, got an elbow hooked onto the window ledge. He knocked the glass out of the window with his other fist, got the window up. And a year or two later—or so it seemed—he was in another bathroom.

A fat woman in a yellow robe stood in the bathroom door. The woman had yellowish hair which had all the attractiveness of binder twine, and she was very thick through hips and bust.

The woman stared at Rush, put up both hands.

"Indians!" she screeched. "Wild Indians!"

She turned and galloped out of the bedroom into the hall. Rush ran after her. The woman looked back, howled, "Indians!" again, and put on more speed.

In the hall, the woman went one direction; Rush went the other. He dived through a door marked with a red "Exit" sign, and found stairs which led downward. He descended with long jumps until he stumbled and fell, then traveled with more care.

When he walked out into the hotel lobby, he tried to breathe regularly and look innocent.

HAD HE not been keeping a sharp lookout for possible trouble, he might not have noticed the newspaper with the small hole in the middle. The hole did not appear quite natural, but looked very much like a hole that someone might have torn in the newspaper to permit a watch to be kept on the elevators and the stairway.

Rush angled over casually, to have a look at whoever might be behind the newspaper.

It was a girl. An Indian girl, and one that was strikingly pretty; small, with interesting curves, long lashes that veiled her eyes, and hair that was fine and not too black. *This*, Rush thought, *is about the prettiest girl I've ever seen, Indian or otherwise.* He went over to her, stood looking down at her.

The girl seemed unaware of his presence. She gave all her attention to the paper.

Putting the paper down on her lap, she bent over it and carefully tore out another small, round piece.

The piece she tore out came from an advertisement; it was the picture of a hat some Tulsa department store was offering for sale.

Either she was absorbed in the subject of hats, or she was clever.

Rush walked out of the hotel. On the sidewalk, he picked the first car that he found open, got in and sat there as though he owned the machine.

He was sitting in the car when the three well-dressed Indians came out of the hotel. They hurried across the sidewalk and sprang into a car. Rush, suddenly realizing he had made a bad move, scrambled out and ran for the trio.

When he realized he could never catch the car containing the Indians, Rush got out of sight behind a parked truck. He watched the trio get away. They had not seen him. The car in which they rode had cost ten thousand dollars if it had cost a cent, he reflected.

He walked to the hotel doorman.

"Who were the three Indians who just left?"

"The three One Arrow boys," the doorman explained. "Sons of the famous old Johnny One Arrow!"

THROUGH THE hotel door, Rush could see enough subdued excitement in the lobby to convince him the shooting and other uproar upstairs was being investigated. Also, he could hear the fat woman saying shrill things about wild Indians. She had a voice as squeaky as ungreased wagon wheels.

Rush sauntered away, walked three blocks, entered a drugstore and bought a remover for the stuff which gave his face its coppery hue.

Next, he went to a men's clothing store, where he bought a suit, shoes, socks, shirt, necktie and hat, all in shades of brown. He liked browns. He changed in the store dressing room.

Stripped, Rush was suddenly not an average man. His body was as wrapped with wiry sinew as the frame of a professional acrobat; he was almost unnaturally muscular. When he twisted to loosen the top on the jar of dye remover, which had stuck, lithe thews stood out incredibly in his arms.

He asked the clothing store clerk, "Ever hear of old Johnny One Arrow?"

"Who hasn't!" the clerk said, surprised.

"What about him?"

"An Osage Indian. Owns half the Osage land around Pawhuska, where oil wells are thicker than pores in your skin."

"Rich, eh?"

"Filthy with it." The clerk absent-mindedly dry-washed his hands at the thought of all the Johnny One Arrow money. "They say he's one of the richest men in the world, only he's got the good sense not to advertise it. Any anyway, he's as stingy as Scrooge, I've heard."

Rush said, "*Ugh,* heap—er—I mean—thanks!"

The street was warm and bright with sunlight, busy with traffic. Standing on a corner waiting for a stop light, Rush saw among the passing vehicles a truckload of oil field pipe, a smaller red truck labeled, "DANGER—NITROGLYC-ERIN!" and four different coupés fitted with bit-rack beds for carrying oil-drilling bits. The rest of the traffic might have been on the street of any city, except that there might be more big cars.

Walking into the hotel lobby, he saw no evidence that anyone recognized him.

There was no sign of the Indian girl who had torn hat advertisements out of a newspaper.

He rode an elevator up to his room.

POLICEMEN STOOD at the room door; more cops were inside.

Then the fat woman came out of the room, looked at Rush and complained shrilly, "They don't believe me, young man! I tell them a wild Indian chased me all over the hotel, and they don't believe me!"

Rush shook his head disapprovingly, said, "Lady, you should beware of the panther sweat these Oklahomans use for liquor."

"The idea! Young man, I've a mind to slap your face!"

She flounced away, muttering about wild Indians and sassy young men.

Rush went to the door of his room.

One of the cops blocked him. "What's eating you?"

"Curiosity," Rush explained.

"Go away. We got enough trouble as is."

Through the hotel room door, Rush saw a man had been examining the contents of the cases which were alike except for size and shape—the cases that contained Rush's equipment. The searcher straightened.

"This stuff," he announced, "seems to belong to somebody named Clickell Rush."

"Find any fingerprints on the stuff in the cases?"

"Sure."

"Photograph them."

Another cop said, "Well, we'd better put out the word to arrest this Clickell Rush for murder."

Rush, outside the door, swallowed hard.

"Murder?" he said.

"G'wan away!" ordered the cop.

Rush went downstairs and located the hotel porter's room, where all heavy baggage entering the hotel was first taken. He was seeking the trunk which had been shipped from Los Angeles by someone.

It was a large, black, metal trunk—and two policemen and two hotel porters were looking at a dead body in the trunk.

CHAPTER III

OSAGE COUNTRY

THE HOTEL BAGGAGE room was warm and quiet, and the four men—the two policemen and the two hotel porters—looking at the body in the trunk, were gripped by that sober silence that seems to come over men in the presence of death.

One of the officers looked around slowly and saw Rush standing in the door.

"Who are you?" he asked in a low voice. "What do you want?"

Rush asked, "Where's the sergeant?"

The trunk lid was standing open, but the trunk was half turned, so that Rush could not see enough of the body in the trunk to tell whether it was white man or redskin, or whether it was male or female. A tweed coat, which covered the part of the body that he could see, might be part of a man's coat, or a woman's. In truth, all he could tell was that there was a form in the trunk; the attitude of the four men told him it was a dead form.

"The sergeant is upstairs," the policeman said.

Rush said, "Thanks. I'll see him first. Then I'll come back."

He backed out of the room, walked from the hotel and strode rapidly along the street. All the muscles in his body, particularly those in his legs, began to feel as though they had been supporting a terrific weight which had been suddenly removed, leaving shaky weakness.

He was accused of murder.

A newsboy directed him to a place that rented trucks. He ran—but not too fast—to the place, and said, "I want to rent a small truck with a closed van body."

"We don't rent them without our own driver," the man said.

"I don't want a driver."

"That's tough, brother. Rent it somewhere else, then."

"Where's another place?"

"Hell, find it yourself!" the man said, and scowled. He was thick and sullen-looking.

"I'll hire it from you," Rush said grimly.

The sullen man drove himself. Rush rode beside him. The truck was old, but efficient, and equipped with a van body, closed by two doors at the rear. It looked secure enough to haul lions.

WHEN THEY had ridden four blocks, Rush reached over suddenly and slapped the driver's cheek.

"Hey!" the driver snarled. "Who you slappin'?"

"You want that mosquito to drink you dry?" Rush asked.

The driver rubbed his cheek with a hand, took the hand away and eyed the drop of crimson on his fingers.

"I oughta bust you one!" he said sourly.

A few more blocks, and the van began to wander over the pavement. Rush took hold of the wheel, guided it, and after a few moments, squirmed over and took the driver's place.

The van driver apparently had gone to sleep.

Rush left him lying in the shade of a tree beside the boulevard which runs along the Arkansas River.

While he drove back to the hotel, Rush refilled the little hypodermic device which fitted one of his fingers like a ring. The drug, which he took from a small phial, was a quick-acting anaesthetic agent, more potent than those used in surgery, and the driver might have a headache when he awakened.

Rush backed the van up to the hotel baggage entrance, then alighted and went into the baggage room. He had his story all ready for the policemen. He had been upstairs, and the sergeant in charge had authorized him to take the body and the trunk to the police station—

But the story was not needed.

The trunk stood, big and black, in the center of the baggage room.

No one was in sight.

The trunk lid was closed, and Rush took hold of it, started to lift it, then took hold of his lower lip tightly with his teeth and released the lid. Death always appalled him, and bodies were something that he hated to look at above all else.

By lifting the trunk, he could tell that there was a body inside.

He carried the trunk to the van, loaded it in the back, closed the doors with the chain arrangement which held them, and got behind the wheel.

He drove away from the hotel with the trunk.

JUDGING BY what sight-seeing he had done from the plane, as it brought him to Tulsa, Rush concluded the most deserted country lay north of town. Driving in that direction, he crossed two sets of railroad tracks, passed block after block of neat bungalows, then climbed a hill which was topped by impressive mansions. After that, there was a rutted dirt road traversing red oak hills.

The Gadget Man drove with brown hat yanked over his eyes, anger in the set of his jaw.

Once, he growled, "I should've known it!"

He meant that he should have known there would be trouble. There always was, when he did anything that was suggested by Bufa, the voice of the toad!

"Blast my own greed!" he added. "And damn those ten-thousand-dollar bills!"

That was it. That was the bait that always got him into these messes. Money had enticed him into coming from Los Angeles, disguised as an Indian named Johnny One Arrow. Greed was responsible.

Two attempts to kill him. Accused of a trunk murder. And he still didn't know what it was all about.

"And if the law catches me with this body," he muttered, "it's liable to be *whango*, the electric chair! Or whatever they use for one in Oklahoma."

But if they didn't catch him, they wouldn't have a body; and it is hard to convict without a *corpus delicti*. It might be used as bait for a trap.

The truck passed a small oil field, one in which the wells were shallow, and where whole groups of wells were pumped by a single chugging engine, being hooked up to the engine by iron rods which sometimes extended for almost a quarter of a mile to reach the pump-jack over some remote well.

Beyond the little oil field, there were more hills. They were very short and steep hills, covered with a more hearty growth of red oaks than had furred the hills nearer Tulsa. Also, in the deep little gullies now were larger trees, cotton-woods and other kinds, and the gully beds were wide and composed of sand and gravel which water had fitted into place so expertly that the beds were almost as level as floors, and packed solidly.

The truck nosed down into the gullies with wheels almost locked, hit the flat gravel beds with a bump, then labored in low gear up the other side.

While on top of a higher hill, Rush looked back. He saw dust, which indicated another car coming behind.

As a matter of caution, he decided to drive up the next gully bed and let the car pass. But no gully bed immediately presented itself; instead, there was a stretch of flat rangeland.

On either side of the road, grader ditches had washed into young canyons which did not look as though they could be crossed by a man on horseback.

Rush was craning his head and looking at the ditches when he heard the plane.

He put his head out to stare. The plane was so close that he dodged involuntarily. It must have come down out of the sky with motor idling almost soundlessly.

Huge and yellow, hurling a great shadow below it, the plane skimmed the top of the truck. The motor snorted a time or two to steady the craft, and it landed on the road ahead and came to a stop. It was a cabin biplane probably ten years old, which made it a decrepit granddaddy, as plane ages go.

The plane appeared to hold a pilot and two passengers. The two passengers got out of the cabin, kneeled on the dusty road and pointed hunting rifles at the truck.

RUSH STOPPED the truck and slid down in the seat until he sat on the floor boards. There, the engine at least protected his stomach from rifle bullets. He had a particular horror of being shot in the stomach.

"All right," one of the men from the plane yelled. "We can throw lead around, or you can be sensible!"

Rush had heard that voice somewhere before.

He shouted, "What the blazes is this, anyway?"

"Get out!"

Rush got out of the truck. The two men with the rifles approached warily, and one searched Rush by slapping a hand over the places where a gun might be concealed.

One of the riflemen was the fellow who had pretended to be a newspaper reporter in Oklahoma City. He did not recognize Rush.

The other man was the driver of the reporter's getaway car in Oklahoma City. At least, he had the same wide shoulders, extraordinarily large fawn-colored cowboy hat and bright bandanna handkerchief.

"Hell, I never saw this guy before!" the reporter growled. He prodded Rush with his gun. "Who are you?"

Rush looked as scared as he could, made his voice shake, and said, "I'm jus—just a guy who was huh-hired to do this."

"Hired to do what?"

"Go to the huh-hotel and slick the cuk-cops out of a trunk."

The reporter nodded. "Yeah. We saw you do that."

The other man was chewing a cigar. He asked, "Who hired you?"

"The One Arrow boys," Rush said, taking a chance.

Both the men laughed.

"That's swell," the reporter said. Evidently he intended to say more, but instead of continuing, he turned his head and stared back along the road. In the distance, the car which had been coming behind Rush had topped a hill. It moved slowly down the hill and disappeared from sight.

"Hey!" the reporter exploded. "That's young One Arrow's car!"

"I think so, too," the other man growled. "We better get that trunk in the plane an' clear out!"

"Hell with the plane!" the reporter snapped. "We'll take this guy and the trunk in the truck, and get on up in the Osage country. Then we'll finish this."

"I don't like—"

"You haven't liked my ideas all along!" the reporter said disgustedly. "That's been the trouble. You're too full of schemes."

The other shrugged. "All right."

THEY MOTIONED to the pilot of the plane to take off. But the aviator got out of the plane and came running back, holding an arm over his face to hide his features.

"Go on—beat it!" the reporter yelled at him. "The job we hired you for is done!"

"I don't want anybody to know about this!" the flier shouted. "Are you sure that truck driver won't identify me later?" The aviator sounded scared.

The reporter said, "This truck driver won't identify anybody. Not where he's goin'."

The aviator, still hiding his face, whirled and raced back to his plane and got in. A moment later the motor roared and the ship picked up its tail and gathered speed.

The plane ran about two hundred feet, then the wheels hit a rut. The craft bounced. It changed its course slightly, and because it did not yet have flying speed, it crashed into the deep ditch beside the road. There was a rending roar as the craft hit, and a cloud of dust arose.

Swearing, the reporter ran toward the plane.

The other man jabbed his rifle at Rush and said, "Lie down!"

Rush lay down. The man came over, took handcuffs out of his pockets and fastened them about Rush's ankles.

"Too bad we ain't got but one set of bracelets," he grumbled.

The reporter had disappeared into the ditch where the plane had crashed. Now he climbed out of the ditch and came running back. As he ran, he doubled over and scooped up handfuls of dust with which he cleaned the stock of his rifle.

"Pilot was trapped in the cockpit," he said.

"Alive?" the other asked.

"Not now." The reporter slapped his rifle stock grimly. "But they'll think the crash caved in his skull."

RUSH WAS thrown into the rear of the truck, alongside the metal trunk. He heard the fastenings of the truck rear doors rattling. The fastener was stout chain, and there was no chance whatever of his breaking out without attracting the notice of the two men in the front seat.

The truck got into motion.

Rush, crowding close to the front partition, listened for whatever the two men had to say to each other. Evidently, one of them stood on the running board and kept a watch on the car behind, because there were sounds indicating he had gotten back inside and slammed the door.

"It's the One Arrows, all right," he shouted over the noise of the truck motor.

"They trying to catch us?" the reporter demanded.

"Don't appear to be. They're just following."

The reporter swore angrily. "They must have been watching that hotel and saw that mug in the back snatch the trunk."

"We didn't notice them."

"Hell, we wouldn't! You know how Indians are."

The truck rolled fast, hit bumps, and Rush braced himself to keep his balance on handcuffed ankles. The trunk bounced around on the truck floor.

"Them One Arrows," the man in the cowboy hat grumbled, "must be figuring on picking their time, then closing in on us."

"That's fine. Let them close in." The reporter sounded fierce and eager. "I can take this rifle and out-shoot any six Indians ever born."

"I don't like—"

"I told you," the reporter yelled, "to shut up about what you don't like! Back there in Los Angeles, we should've just shot old Johnny One Arrow and let 'em think a burglar done it. Only you had to get smart ideas!"

THE MAN in the cowboy hat grumbled discontentedly. "But I wanted the whole family wiped out!"

"Yeah? And look what happened! We put the body in a trunk, and ship it to Tulsa by air express."

The reporter swore for a while.

"Then we learn somebody is flying to Tulsa under the name of Johnny One Arrow," he continued. "So we're plenty puzzled, and we smell big rats without knowing what kind. And we try to kill this fake Johnny One Arrow in Oklahoma City, and don't."

"If you had gone ahead and shot him with that trick camera—"

"Damn you, don't you go blaming me! I did my best!"

The other man said peevishly, "It was your idea, changing the address on the trunk, and sending it to the fake Johnny One Arrow in Tulsa. You said the killing would be framed on him automatically. That went wrong, didn't it?"

"Dammit, how was I to know the One Arrow boys would start looking for their old man's body? Who tipped them?"

"Well, who did?"

The reporter yelled, "Oh, how the hell do I know? Maybe that guy dressed up like a circus Indian, who booked plane passage from Los Angeles as Johnny One Arrow. The guy we tried to kill in Oklahoma City. *Who was that guy?*"

"That fellow in back can hear you, the way you're yelling!"

"Let him hear! He won't be telling anybody."

The conversation ended with that, however, and Rush stood for some time, braced against motion of the truck, and listened without hearing anything more.

He hobbled back and sat on the trunk, sat there for some time, trying to tell himself he should take a look at the body of old Johnny One Arrow. But he could not stand bodies; they filled him with horror. He should have looked at the body at the hotel, and he hadn't wanted to; he should look at it now, and he still didn't want to.

But after he had fought his own mind for a while, he unfastened the trunk and lifted the lid.

The gun which looked him in the eyes was small and bright, like the Indian girl who held the weapon.

CHAPTER IV
THE FAT WOMAN

NATURE HAS PROVIDED all living creatures with an instinctive reaction to surprise, and instilled the thing into them so deeply that it is almost impossible to defy it. Animals, birds and reptiles all move suddenly when surprised, and the instinct extends to man as well. Rush jumped, surprised by what he had found in the trunk, and because his ankles were handcuffed, he fell down.

The Indian girl got half out of the trunk, to keep her gun pointed at him. She was the same very attractive young woman who had been tearing hat pictures out of a newspaper in the lobby of the Tulsa hotel. But the girl actually had been watching him through a hole in her newspaper, Rush knew now.

She peered at him, particularly at the handcuffs which secured his ankles. The handcuffs seemed to change all her ideas.

"Who's driving the truck?" she whispered.

"Two men. One claimed to be a newspaper reporter. The other one wears a cowboy hat."

"Short, thick man?"

"The one with the hat, yes."

"Big Hat Weeks," she said grimly. "The other one really used to be a reporter. They pal around together."

She sank back in the trunk and half closed the lid. "Can they see me now?"

"No."

"I may be able to shoot the links of your leg manacles in two."

Rush shook his head. "I don't want any woman shooting at my feet. I'll get loose when the time comes." He got close to the trunk, so that his whisper would carry. "Who are you?"

"I'm Edna One Arrow."

"Johnny One Arrow—"

"My father," the girl said in a low voice.

Rush looked at her closely, and revised the somewhat skeptical ideas he had held hitherto about the legendary stoicism of the American Indian in the face of suffering.

"I'm Clickell Rush," he explained. "I'm a—well, a detective without portfolio, sort of."

"Who hired you?"

"A toad."

The girl looked at him queerly. "Toad?"

"Skip it. Go on with your story." She shook her head.

"A crazy man!" she said. "And I was afraid the whole terrible thing was the work of a crazy man."

THE TRUCK stopped then, and Rush realized he had lost valuable time. He doubled down quickly and felt in his left trousers cuff for the slender steel which he had threaded into the fabric when he had dressed in the clothing store. He got hold of the wire—it was less stiff than a needle, but had the same probing qualities—and went to work on the handcuff lock. He picked frantically.

When the truck doors opened, he was lying on the floor with the manacles still in place on his ankles.

"Drag him out," the reporter ordered.

Rush looked at the trunk. The girl had disappeared inside and closed the lid.

"Big Hat" Weeks hauled Rush out of the truck, got the Gadget Man over his shoulder, and walked toward a house.

The house was the last kind of structure Rush had expected to see here in these red oak hills; a brick house, low and rambling and exquisitely designed after the English style of architecture.

The house did not look as if it were being lived in.

But two tepees near by did look as if they were lived in.

The combination of a splendid but uninhabited house and a tepee that was being used, puzzled Rush—until he remembered reading something about such doings in a Sunday magazine feature somewhere. It seemed that the oil-rich redskins of Oklahoma did such queer things as erecting grandly furnished houses in the Osage hills, then disdained to live in them, inhabiting instead their tepees—which they erected in the front yards.

BIG HAT WEEKS dumped Rush on the floor inside the front door of the house.

"Help me with this trunk!" the reporter called.

They came stumbling in under the weight of the trunk, which they put down near Rush.

"Now what's next?" Big Hat Weeks demanded uneasily.

"When we shipped old Johnny One Arrow's body from Los Angeles, our idea was to frame his murder onto his sons, wasn't it?" the reporter demanded.

"Yes. Only—"

"Only a mystery man Johnny One Arrow turned up, so we thought we'd frame him by sending him the body of the real Johnny One Arrow."

"That fell through."

"All right. Here's what we do now." The reporter pointed at Rush. "We scrag all the One Arrows and frame it on the wise guy, here."

Big Hat Weeks looked at Rush and shook his head. "The law wouldn't swallow that. They'd say he didn't have any motive for knocking off the One Arrow family."

"Motive—hell!" The reporter laughed grimly. "I've figured out who this guy is."

Big Hat pointed at Rush. "Why, he's a truck—"

"Truck driver—nothing. *He's the other Johnny One Arrow!*"

"The other—" Big Hat Weeks made a gulping sound, and his mouth remained open.

"See how it stacks?" the reporter demanded gleefully. "He murdered old Johnny One Arrow in Los Angeles, brought the body here. The One Arrow family trailed him. They had a fight, and everybody got killed."

Big Hat Weeks pointed at Rush. "But who is he?"

"We don't care who he is."

They crouched down at the door and a window with their rifles, and waited for the One Arrows to come.

IT WAS now near evening, and the sunlight was red and warm, while under the eaves of the house, swallows made gentle sounds as they went in and out of their mud nests. There was a slight breeze, and this rustled the leaves of the red oaks which crowded close to the dwelling.

Inside the house, it was distressingly still. The air was like the air inside a furniture store; filled with the odors associated with new furniture and new rugs, for the rooms had not been lived in enough to take away newness. None of the furniture had been soiled, and none of it showed signs of use. The paint on the walls was bright and unspotted, but spiders had fashioned entanglements of gray webs in the corners.

The reporter began, "They should've showed up by—"

He stopped and grew tense.

The other man grew tense also, pressed his cheek against the rifle stock, the fatty looseness of his cheek bulging above the polished walnut of the stock.

There was the sound of a car with a good motor coming close to the house.

Rush took the handcuffs off his ankles. He had succeeded in picking the locks previously with the wire.

The reporter said, "Let's blaze away!"

Rush threw the handcuffs.

They hit the reporter; he barked, went forward on his knees, and his rifle smacked deafeningly.

Rush, leaping as he threw the cuffs, landed on Big Hat. His hands clamped on Big Hat's rifle. Big Hat reared up with Rush across his shoulders, hanging to the rifle. Rush banded his legs around the man's ample middle.

The reporter had let fall his rifle. On hands and knees, he shook his head, clearing it. Then he clutched the rifle, felt uncertainly for the trigger and wheeled around, still on all fours, toward Rush.

The girl got out of the trunk. She started for the reporter with high hopes; but she was cramped from being in the trunk, and when she kicked at his rifle, her foot missed the weapon entirely and the high heel of her shoe peeled the side of his face. Momentum of the missed kick tipped the girl off balance, so that she fell, half turning as she went down, and her head whacked the wall very hard. The concussion of her head against the wall stunned her; she did not move after she hit the floor.

RUSH FOUGHT with his own foe, and they got against the wall. Rush, still on the man's back, put both feet against the wall, pushed hard, and the two of them hit the reporter, who was about to get organized with his rifle. The three tied up in a two-wrestlers-and-a-referee knot.

Rush began to think that the stuff from the little hypodermic ring was never going to take effect on either foe. He wore the ring; he had fanged each opponent repeatedly, but they went on fighting.

He got the range of a stomach, and pounded away. One rifle flew out of the mêlée. The other one followed. They hit the walls noisily. There was a moment when they were all locked together and straining, and in that drawn silence when muscles were as tight as fiddle strings, Rush could hear disturbed swallows beating wings and crying outside.

Then Big Hat Weeks went to sleep. A little later, the reporter did likewise.

Rush listened. It was too quiet outdoors.

From a pocket, Rush took a metal cigarette case. This held cigarettes. He counted three from the right, took all three cigarettes and broke them open.

The cigarettes were wadded at each end with tobacco, and the central portion contained small, grayish pellets. The pellets were about pinhead size, and had somewhat the aspect of worthless pearls. From the three cigarettes, Rush got a small heap of the pellets in the palm of his hand.

He sent the pellets across the floor with a tiny rattling. They scattered, and when they stopped rolling, lay all around the spot where Rush sat.

In a moment, the One Arrows came in. The first one in lifted a cocked rifle, pointed it at Rush.

"**WAIT A** minute!" barked one of the brothers. "There's no hurry."

The Indian with the rifle snarled, "He killed dad. Now he's killed sister, Big Hat and that reporter."

"There's still no hurry."

The third Indian came in, and the trio of them stood just inside the door, holding their rifles on Rush.

Rush said, "Wouldn't you like to know the motive for all these killings?"

"You're damn right!" gritted the One Arrow who was named Andy.

"So would I," Rush said.

They stared at him.

Andy said, "Let's kick the truth out of him."

The idea got instant approval. They started for Rush.

"Keep away from me!" Rush yelled.

The shout did what he thought it would do—made them jump for him more rapidly. And as they came for him, it was impossible for their feet to miss the tiny pellets which Rush had spread over the floor. When the first foot came down on a pellet, it exploded.

Probably the pellet blast was no greater than a giant firecracker. But surprise gave it the violence of dynamite. The Indian howled, lifted in the air, came down—and two pellets exploded this time. The other two One Arrow brothers jumped in to help, got on the little pellets, and the house interior took on the sound effects of a Fourth of July.

Rush heaved up, got one of the rifles away from its owner and began whipping heads with the rifle barrel.

THE MAN from the Indian agency—it had developed that he took charge in a matter of this kind, instead of the sheriff—was a long, grizzled individual in high-heeled boots. He had an old-fashioned handle-bar mustache which, judging from its appearance, was frequently masticated along with his chewing tobacco.

He appeared from another part of the Indian agency offices, produced his plug of tobacco, took a chew, then offered it to Rush, who declined.

"Nobody got hurt bad," he said. "But I guess they'll hang Big Hat and the reporter. That's too bad."

"Whether it's too bad is a matter of opinion," Rush said.

Edna One Arrow came in, smiled at Rush, then took a chair.

"They believe my story, even if it is pretty wild," she explained. "You see, when my father disappeared in Los Angeles, I called a detective agency. They must have notified someone else, because another voice called me back, and asked for all particulars—"

"This voice give a name?" Rush asked.

"Bufa."

Rush winced, said, "Remember that toad I told you about?"

"Yes. I thought you were crazy."

"The toad's voice is named Bufa."

The girl looked at him queerly. "That doesn't seem sensible."

"I'll say it doesn't make sense," Rush said sourly. "But go on. What happened?"

"I learned a trunk had been shipped air express to Tulsa. I also learned a man using my father's name had booked plane passage. So I came to Tulsa. My brothers and I began investigating. I saw you hire that truck and knew what you planned. The police had taken my—my father's body from the trunk, and left the trunk.

"So I got in it and you took me. I did that because I figured you would take the body to whoever had hired you to do the killing. As a matter of fact, I suspected Big Hat Weeks was back of the whole thing, and that it was a plan to wipe out our whole family."

"You suspected Big Hat?"

"Yes."

"Why?"

"My father," the Indian girl said, "was very rich. And he was wise; He knew money ruins my people, so he never gave his children more than a hundred dollars a month apiece."

"I don't see what that—"

"I have an invalid sister," Edna One Arrow said.

"Eh?"

"Big Hat Weeks is married to my sister." The girl put her face in her hands.

The Indian agent got up and cleared his throat noisily.

"You see, partner," he explained, "it was just a case of a no-account squaw man killin' a passel of his wife's relatives—so she'd inherit."

IT WAS well on into the following day before Rush got back to Tulsa and convinced the police, with the aid of the Indian agent, that it really was a case of a man killing off relatives, so that his invalid wife would inherit Osage oil millions. The police finally accepted that much of the story.

They never would, it became apparent, accept the idea that Rush was involved in the thing because there was a toad that talked.

Rush gave up trying to explain, went back to his hotel and listened to the management complain about the bullet holes in the walls.

Later, a bellhop appeared with a package.

"The lady next door left this for you," the bellboy explained.

"Oh, I remember," Rush said. "That was the fat lady who had wild-Indian trouble."

The package contained a woman's dress, a padded contraption to give a man's hips the shape of a fat woman's, and another contraption to do the same for his chest. There was a bristling binder-twine-colored wig—the hair that had been worn by the fat woman next door.

There was also a paper, on which writing said:

WHAT DO YOU THINK OF ME AS A FAT
GIRL?
BUFA.

Pinned to the note was the other half of the ten-thousand-dollar bank note.

THE ITCHING MEN

IT WAS NICE WORK AND THE GADGET
MAN GOT IT FOR TEN GRAND—IF
HE COULD SAVE A CONDEMNED
MAN FROM THE CHAIR!

CHAPTER I

GHOST WITH NIPPERS

THE GOVERNOR OF the state was superstitious. He practically believes in ghosts.

That explained a lot.

It explained how Clickell Rush came to be sitting on top of a telephone pole as the clock on the village courthouse struck the ungodly hour of midnight.

Perched on top of the telephone pole, Rush looked, he rather suspected, like an owl. Most owls are brown, and Rush preferred to wear all his clothes in shades of browns; so he thought it was appropriate to think of an owl. He was tempted to hoot and see how it sounded.

However, while he was hooting, a man might die.

Also it was obvious that straddling the topmost crossarm of a telephone pole at the stroke of midnight, and hooting like an owl, was a procedure naked of dignity. It was also shy on common sense. It lacked any kind of sense at all.

Rush had to keep telling himself it was not as crazy as it looked.

Moreover, nobody would ever know.

This was going to be a secret. Just this once, he would keep it to himself. Not a word if it was going to get into the newspapers.

The newspapers had a habit of blatting out his doings for everybody to read and—Rush strongly suspected—laugh at. Clickell Rush, the "Gadget Man" was excellent printing-press fodder. The things he did had that whacky touch which reads well in print; for instance: Sitting on a telephone pole at dark midnight.

But this once, he'd fool the newspapers; they weren't going to know a thing about this night's doings.

They could think it was the work of spooks.

The governor of the state certainly had to believe that spooks had functioned. A man's life depended on it.

"Here goes," Rush remarked.

He had brought along a jointed pole, a pole that was of a hard rubber composition, stronger than wood. To one end of this pole was fastened a nipper which could cut through very thick wire. From the nipper handle, a cord ran to the other end of the pole, a strong cord that was a nonconductor of electricity. The whole thing was a wire-cutter.

Rush reached out and hooked the wire-cutter onto the high-tension electric power line. He could just reach the high-tension wires from the top of the telephone pole. The line carried he-didn't-know-how-many thousand volts of electricity and if the pole and the cord hadn't been a nonconductor of electricity, doubtless Rush would have been killed instantly.

Probably the electricity would have slain him as quickly as it was going to kill the man named Jonathan Noble in the electric chair at the State penitentiary.

Or rather, like it would electrocute Jonathan Noble if the governor of the state didn't happen to be sufficiently superstitious.

Now Rush could cut the power line any time he wanted. **THE ELECTRIC** high-line was the only one that ran to the State penitentiary. It fed current to the prison lights, to machines in the overall factory, broom factory and to devices for stamping automobile license plates; all these activities being located inside the penitentiary walls, along with the big generator which converted current from the high-tension line into the most suitable kind of juice for taking a man's life. The electric chair stood in a room all its own.

In the room with the electric chair were now assembled about fifteen men. They were waiting to see Jonathan Noble die.

Ten of the spectators were in various stages of drunkenness. They were newspaper reporters. And newspaper reporters almost always get drunk when they have to see an electrocution. It is supposed to make it easier.

"He still claims he's innocent," one reporter muttered.

"I wish it was over," croaked another.

The warden said, "Bring him in."

The word went back to the death cell where Jonathan Noble had been talking to the chaplain.

"Bring him in."

Two penitentiary guards gripped Jonathan Noble's arms. One guard walked ahead, followed by the chaplain, and four guards followed behind; and every man in the procession had his lips pressed tightly together and took each step in a slow, conscious way.

There is something about leading a condemned man to the death room that makes you think about your own mind and your own body, and wonder what gave you the right to turn God and take away the life of a human. You wonder what will be done about it later on, when your earthly total is added up. You try to think, "Well, the court and the judge ordered this, and they've got a guy in there who gets a hundred dollars for throwing the switch, so it's really not my fault." But thinking that way doesn't help much.

A pin could *not* have been heard dropping as the death march reached the black room which had the one grim piece of furniture, but that was because the generator in an adjoining room was making too much noise. The generator was humming loudly.

They put a stereotyped question to condemned men before they kill them.

"Have you anything to say?"

Jonathan Noble stood straight. He looked like a young man who would always stand straight, no matter what hardships befell him. He was tall; his jaw and his shoulders were square. He appeared to be a nice two-fisted young man with a clean mind and a pure heart.

The prosecuting attorney for the state had made him out a two-fisted devil-may-care with nerves of steel. But then, the prosecuting attorney was coming up soon for election as mayor. He hadn't presented any really tangible proof that Jonathan Noble had a black character.

But with all the circumstantial evidence they'd had against Jonathan Noble, they hadn't needed anything else to send him to the electric chair.

The warden repeated his question.

"Have you anything to say?"

Jonathan Noble stood straighter. He lifted both his arms slowly. His fists clenched.

"I am innocent," he said. "But if you are to believe that, the proof must come from some omen, I suppose."

He stood there, very still, with his arms lifted rigidly.

"There must be a Power that saves innocent ones," he added in a low voice.

And then, as if the invisible Power had come to his aid—as though the ethereal cavalry had galloped up to save him at the last minute—the electric generator moan faltered.

The lights grew dim, went black.

There was utter stillness in the room of death.

"The omen!" a reporter croaked.

Said the more practical warden, "The blasted power has failed."

Yes, the power had failed. They telephoned the substation and learned nothing could be done about it, because the high-line carrying the juice had parted. The substation men explained that they had dispatched their linemen, but it might be hours before the trouble was corrected.

The warden telephoned the governor. Jonathan Noble was supposed to die between midnight and one o'clock, and the warden wanted to know what to do about it.

The governor of the state listened intently to all the warden said. Then the governor asked questions. Particularly, he was interested in the ghostly aspects of the power failure.

"I grant the condemned Jonathan Noble," said the governor finally, "a one-week stay of execution. He will not be electrocuted until one week from today—if nothing else happens."

The governor of the state was superstitious. That he often went to seances given by professional mediums was a fact a great many people knew.

CLICKELL RUSH was one of those who knew how superstitious the governor was.

Rush still sat on top of the telephone pole, but now he felt rather more like an angel than an owl. He had cut a wire and saved a life. There is nothing like saving a life to make a man feel good.

It was not the first life Click Rush had preserved, but that did not keep him from feeling angelic over having done it again.

True, he had not witnessed the events in the penitentiary, but he knew the exact time the electrocution was scheduled, and he knew that with no current there couldn't very well be an electrocution; and he also knew enough about the governor to bet his bottom dollar that the superstitious executive would give the condemned man a reprieve.

Also, Click Rush, at the moment, was hating to think of sliding down the telephone pole to the earth. He had dropped one of his climbing spurs, hence the only way to get down the pole was slide. The pole had splinters, he suspected.

By rights, he should have left the top of the pole long before now. But he had remained perched, feeling angelic, and thinking of splinters.

Click Rush was an average-size man, but he was very muscular. He was frequently mistaken for a circus acrobat by people accustomed to knowing circus acrobats when they saw them.

Moreover, according to the newspapers, Rush also had brains. He was an inventor, and he had concocted over ten thousand unique gadgets for catching crooks, gadgets so unique that he had not been able to sell them to any police departments. The only way he seemed to be able to make any money out of his unusual gadgets was use them himself, which he had been doing for several months. As a result, the newspapers had conceded that he had brains.

Muscle and brains he might have, but still the only way to get down from the telephone pole was to slide.

He said, "Whew!"

He was referring to the splinters.

It was too dark to see the climbing spur he had dropped. The night was so black that the surrounding woods were nodulose wads of sepia, and the concrete highway near by was only a faintly gray ribbon, while Rush's car on the road was a box-shaped shadow. Somewhere in the distance, a farm dog was baying; but there certainly wasn't any moon to encourage the canine.

Rush reflected again that it was a fool business to be sitting on top of a telephone pole at the hour of midnight.

But nobody would ever know.

Rush set himself to slide.

Instead, he came within an ace of jumping right off the top of the telephone pole.

When lightning strikes, there is noise. This time, there was only a flash. A white flash—so white as to be utterly blinding. It couldn't very well be lightning.

The flash lasted almost as long as it takes to snap two fingers together. But it was completely blinding. There was no sound.

Rush hung to the telephone pole for dear life. His knees knocked against the pole. The white flash of light had surprised him so much that he had all but jumped off, and it was a thirty-foot telephone pole and there was a thorn thicket below. So his knees knocked the pole.

After a while, he slid down.

He looked all around the vicinity with a flashlight. Having found nothing, he started telling himself that the snipped electric power line wires *might* have short-circuited with the ground and made a flash as white and as brilliant as that one.

But he couldn't quite sell himself that idea.

He drove away in his car, talking to himself, principally about the splinters.

Thank blazes, nobody would ever know about them.

CHAPTER II
SO NOBODY KNEW!

CLICKELL RUSH HAD taken a two-year lease on an apartment. The place had four rooms, and he had decorated two chambers in modernistic style for comfortable living; and two of the rooms he had rigged up as a workshop and laboratory, where he intended to do some more inventing.

He was hoping to invent something sensible, so that he could sell it to a police department. He intended to endeavor to restrain his impulse to invent fantastic gadgets. The apartment was equipped with a number of his devices, and he liked everything in the place, with one exception.

The thing he didn't like was the toad named "Bufa."

Bufa, the toad, had warts. Bufa was green on the back and muddy-looking underneath, and could sit in a medium-size suitcase and still leave room for a little cotton packing all around. Bufa's skeleton was brass, his hide of papier-mâché composition.

Bufa's entrails were coils, vacuum tubes, and the rest of the parts of a compact wired-radio "transceiver." The toad could transmit and receive conversation over the city's electric light system.

It was merely necessary to insert a lighted electric light bulb in Bufa's mouth. The heat from the bulb closed a thermostat, and this switched on the apparatus, all ready to function.

Rush put a lighted bulb in the toad's mouth.

He leaned close to the ear of the thing. The microphone was in the toad's left ear, the loud-speaker in the roof of its mouth.

"I resign!" Rush said.

"*You what?*"

The toad's voice was obviously disguised, probably by the speaker keeping two fingers in his or her mouth.

"I quit."

"*But,*" said the toad, "*you've just got started.*"

"I'm turned around and going the other direction." Rush glared at the toad. "Beginning now, I have nothing more to do with this business."

"*Haven't you got a heart?*"

"My heart pumps red and white corpuscles through my body," Rush explained grimly. "It is only poets who are guided by their hearts. Mine does practical work."

"*You're hard-hearted! You'd let an innocent man die in the electric chair.*"

"Didn't the governor give him a stay of execution?"

"*Yes,*" the voice of the toad admitted. "*But Jonathan Noble isn't out of the penitentiary yet.*"

"Why should he be? A judge and a jury put him in there legally."

Rush grew indignant. It was easy for him to work up a stew while talking to the toad. Nothing he had ever known had aggravated him like this silly toad.

Rush yelled, "What makes you think Jonathan Noble is innocent?"

"*I just have a hunch,*" the toad said.

Rush made an angry swiping gesture at his own ears.

"I'm full up to here on your hunches!" he shouted.

NO PRIVATE detective, Rush thought heatedly, had ever been hired by an employer as dizzy as this one. Likewise,

Rush wondered if he wasn't the first private detective in history to solve a string of fantastic crimes without having any idea who had hired him. It made his temper give off sparks to think about it.

Months ago, he'd found a toad sitting on half a ten-thousand-dollar bank note in his hotel room, along with instructions about how to use the thing. When Rush tuned in, the disguised voice had told him, *"I am Bufa, of the species* Bufonidæ, *and I feed on slugs and insects—of the human variety."*

Crazy as a bat, Rush had thought.

The voice of Bufa had had a hunch that a crime had been committed, unknown to the police—and the voice had wanted Rush to use his gadgets to solve the crime. Because ten thousand dollars was real folding money, Rush had turned private detective and solved the case, and gotten the other half of the bank note.

For months now, Rush had been trying to stop being a detective, but a ten-thousand-dollar bill, or some other bait, was always defeating him.

In this present case, Bufa's hunch was that a man named Jonathan Noble was innocent.

Rush did not know anything about Jonathan Noble, except that the newspapers said he was to be executed for the murder of a man named Romero Enterline.

Rush had found the usual half of a ten-thousand-dollar bill under Bufa, and he had connected up, and Bufa's voice had told him that his new job was to stop the electrocution of Jonathan Noble. That had been only this afternoon, so Rush had been too busy in the meantime to think of anything but a method of stopping the execution. Having succeeded, he considered the job done.

Rush had been looking away from the toad and thinking. He could not think when he was looking at the thing.

"You've got a faculty for spotting a crime," he admitted grudgingly. "Call it hunch, or whatever you want."

"I believe I have a supernatural gift for spotting a wrong that has been done," the toad said.

"I believe you're nuts," Rush said.

"I am wealthy," the toad continued unperturbed, *"and few things entertain me. I enjoy seeing wrongs righted. However, being a great physical coward, I much prefer looking on to taking part in any excitement. That is why I hire you."*

He had told Bufa he did not have a heart, but this must be an exaggeration, because something inside him was making him want to go ahead and learn whether Jonathan Noble was innocent, and if he was, to save him.

Rush felt that here was a case he would tackle because he wanted to, not because of Bufa's ten thousand dollars. He had yelled that quitting talk at Bufa just to keep in form.

"All right," he said. "I'll go ahead."

Bufa's voice turned astonished. *"You will save Jonathan Noble if he is innocent?"*

"I'll try."

Bufa made a clucking noise of regret. *"I guess I had better apologize."*

"Apologize for what?"

"The dirty trick I done you."

"Eh?"

"I figured," Bufa said, *"that you wouldn't want to take another case for me."*

"Well?"

"So I took measures to embarrass you into going ahead with the case."

Rush yelled, "What the blasted blankety-blank do you mean—embarrass?"

"Go buy a late newspaper," Bufa said regretfully.

RUSH WENT out and bought the newspaper, and his ears got red.

The picture on the front page was very good. The focus was perfect. Clarity was remarkable. The photographic composition was excellent. And the news value would be hard to excel. If that picture did not win a prize competition somewhere, there would be something wrong.

It showed Clickell Rush, the Gadget Man, sitting on top of the telephone pole near the hour of midnight.

"But nobody was to know about that!" Rush said hollowly.

The picture had been taken by means of the bright flash which had nearly startled Rush into leaping off the telephone pole. The photographer had then sneaked away silently into the night. Also, the photographer had been on the spot because of a telephone tip to trail Clickell Rush and see what developed. The cut lines below the photograph contained this information.

Rush knew that the voice of Bufa, the toad, had telephoned the tip to the picture man.

The story with the picture clarified other points. There was a statement by the governor of the state, a bitter one. The governor had been told by the newspaper that the "omen" which had led him to postpone the electrocution of Jonathan Noble, had been nothing else but a man named Clickell Rush cutting the electric power line.

Said the governor's statement:

> The sovereign rights of this state have been invaded by the man named Clickell Rush. Quite plainly, he has broken the law.
>
> I have issued orders to find Clickell Rush and arrest him.

RUSH GRITTED, "The political clown!"

He leaned against a lamp post beside the newsstand where he had bought the paper, and thought violent things about the governor. Then he read the rest of the story. Down toward the end, the executive's statement said:

> In view of the strange aspects of this matter, the reprieve of Jonathan Noble will stand. Noble will not be executed for one week.

Rush amended, "Maybe the governor isn't so clowny, at that."

The Gadget Man continued to lean against the lamp post for some time, painting a complete mental picture of the bear he seemed to be holding by the tail.

"This thing is screwy and complicated," he said grimly. "I've got to keep it simple. Let's see now—"

He had stopped the execution of a condemned man by a trick, and for that he was going to be arrested.

There was a few hours less than one week in which to learn whether the condemned man was innocent or guilty, and if innocent, get him out of the death cell.

In order to keep from being arrested, the first thing for Rush to do was get away from his apartment, and go into hiding. He'd better take such gadgets as he might need.

"There it is, all in a nutshell," Rush said doubtfully. "And quite simple it is, too."

CHAPTER III
THE WORDY WENCH

THE SCIENCE OF electricity, without argument, is an advanced art, and any technical explanation of one of its devices is jammed with such terms as microfarads, lines of force, impedence and henries, these being words which confuse an average individual.

But for that matter, the automobile sharks use a technical jargon composed of such terms as octane ratings, rypoids and torques, but such things are not necessary to know that an automobile runs.

By the same reasoning, anyone who has ever tuned in an old-time radio receiver knows that the contraption will whistle if a hand is brought close. Hence that human body coming near a certain type of electrical circuit will cause a whistle. If the electric circuit is connected up with a mesh of fine wires under rugs in rooms, anyone standing in any of the rooms will cause the whistle. If the receiver doing the whistling is hidden behind the mail box outside, and turned on simply by pushing hard against the mail box, that makes it convenient.

That was how Rush knew there was an invader in his apartment.

Rush got down on his knees, took a mechanical pencil out of his pocket, put the point of the pencil into the keyhole, then worked the cap of the pencil like a small pump. This injected tear gas silently into the apartment.

A little tear gas will go a long way on closed rooms.

There was an ornate brass knocker on the door. Rush carefully lifted this off, and held it ready to tap the skull of anyone driven out of the apartment by the tear gas. The knocker had been designed for exactly that purpose.

Almost everybody has had the feeling that he would like to have a club in hand when walking into his darkened home, and Rush had supplied himself with this door knocker for such occasions.

Nobody came out of the apartment.

Later, Rush went in.

She lay face-down across Rush's bed, and she was so rigid that at first he thought she was dead; so that he had a devil-size vision of trying to explain a dead girl in his apartment to the police, on top of the telephone-pole-at-midnight thing.

Then she began kicking her feet. She kicked them like a swimmer in a race. She gave out hissing noises and words. The words were foreign.

Rush went around in front of her and saw that her face was very pretty; also that she had been carrying a gun, but had put it down on the floor while she rubbed her tear-gas-irritated eyes.

She had not heard Rush. He dived, and got the gun. She stopped kicking and hissing. She was too blinded to be able to see him effectively.

Rush opened the windows and turned on electric fans. His own eyes were wet and stinging, but the gas was weak enough by now that it had not blinded him.

When he went back, the girl was feeling around on the floor for her gun, which was in Rush's pocket.

"What say," Rush suggested, "that we get acquainted?"

They had a fight. The girl was off the floor and around his neck before he got his mouth closed. Rush immediately made a mistake. Past experience had told him that women either bit you, scratched you, or pulled your hair. He put a hand up quickly to protect his hair.

But this girl knew jiu-jitsu, or something worse. She took hold of Rush in different places, and did not keep her holds long, but it felt as if she had six-inch knives for fingers.

Rush was very glad to get her locked in a closet.

He started to put the closet key in his pocket.

"I'll take the key," a strange voice said.

RUSH LOOKED at him, said, "I guess you may, at that."

The man came in—and Rush made a mental note to put some kind of an attachment on the fire escape to show when it was occupied.

The man was not a Negro. It must be the utter whiteness of his hair which gave that impression, at first. His features were not Negroid; they were finely chiseled. His age, judging from the amount of flesh on his body more than anything else, might be near sixty.

The man stepped to one side.

Four more men came through the window behind him. They were very smooth, very serious-looking young men who must have come, Rush decided, from South America.

The revolvers they held, however, were of a United States make noted for efficiency.

"I bring company, you see," said the older man.

Rush scowled. "Humorist, eh?"

The white-haired man smiled. He had a fancy for gold in his dental work. Smiling, he suddenly made Rush think of an old snow-headed buzzard who had been picking gold, not flesh, off men's bones, and some of it had stuck in his teeth.

"I doubt if I'm a humorist," the man said. "But I'm very happy at this moment."

"That's nice."

"You are the Gadget Man, aren't you?"

"According to the newspapers."

"We have heard of you."

Rush said, "Which adds up to what?"

"It explains," the white-headed man said, "why we were shocked to learn you have apparently decided to prove that Jonathan is not guilty of the crime of which he was convicted."

Rush looked incredulous, and demanded, "What on earth gave you such an idea?"

The other showed his gold-spotted teeth. "We're not dumb."

"You're certainly not behaving so it makes sense."

The white-haired man said, "Search him, *caballeros*. Search him good."

They surrounded Rush very carefully, and went through his pockets; but they found nothing except some silver coins and a billfold containing small bank notes and one half of a ten-thousand-dollar bill.

Seeming surprised that they had not found more, they returned the stuff to Rush's pockets.

"We wouldn't want you to be found dead with empty pockets," the white-haired man said. "Someone might think it was robbery."

Rush swallowed. Sometimes he suspected he could get several times as scared as an average man.

The man turned to the others. "See if you can find the stuff which he used to cut the power line."

They searched and made a pile on the table of the climbing spurs and jointed wire-cutter pole which Rush had employed.

Rush said, "I don't get this."

"You're going to fall off a telephone pole," the other explained, "and break your neck."

The girl had been extremely quiet in the closet.

"Get her out," the man said.

One of the raiders opened the closet door.

The fellow who had opened the door put his hands to his throat and walked backward from the closet, taking steps as if he were drunk, and getting drunker with each step.

The girl was lying huddled in the closet. She was perfectly motionless, but did not seem unconscious, for her eyes were open.

"What the blazes!" ejaculated the white-haired man.

RUSH WENT into action then. It seemed as good a time as any. He clutched at his own throat and looked as horrified as he could.

"Maybe the girl broke the container of poison gas in that closet!" he croaked. "I had one stored there!"

Then he flopped over on his side and lay stiffly.

The men were horrified. The leader jumped and seized the one who had first opened the closet. This man was now on the point of giving up and lying down.

"Gas!" the afflicted one managed to croak.

The leader yelled, "Put your guns away, you fools! And give me a hand with him!"

They shoved their weapons into pockets, and obediently helped hold up the man who had opened the closet.

"Let's get out of here!" a man gasped wildly.

"Shoot that damned Rush first!" their chief ordered.

Rush had been afraid of something like that. So he had carefully taken hold of the rug with both hands. The rug was soft enough that he got very satisfactory handfuls. He jerked, and there was a general upsetting.

Unfortunately, the floor was slicker than he had anticipated, and a moment later he was flat on his back holding the whole rug, and his opponents were picking themselves up off the floor.

Rush came to his feet, snatched the girl out of the closet and raced for a door. He got through the door just as a bullet hit the floor and sent a shower of splinters after him.

Rush was now in one of the work rooms. He seized a bottle off one of the chemical racks. The bottle contained about a gallon of yellowish liquid.

Rush hurled the bottle into the room with the men, and it broke on the floor.

Then Rush slammed the door and snapped the lock, after which he felt much better. All the doors were bulletproof, or so the salesman from the steel company had told him.

The men thumped the door, yelled some horrifying threats, and fired bullets at the lock. They had no luck. Then, frightened by the talk of gas and the yellowish stuff from the bottle—it was steaming all over the floor—they fled through the apartment window and down the fire escape.

Rush, grimacing at the way he had neglected to fortify the fire escape, got a container of tear gas. But by the time he reached a window with this, the enemy had gained the ground.

When he put his head out, they shot the glass from the window immediately above. Rush promptly ducked back.

"Watch the newspaper want ads!" he yelled, as loud as he could.

After that advice, he retreated to another room, on the chance the apartment house walls might not be bulletproof.

Hearing a car leave the vicinity, he presumed the foe had taken flight.

He also heard a neighbor put his head out of a window and yell, "Telephone the police, somebody!"

"I've already done it!" shouted another voice.

Rush ignored the yellowish vapor that was coming like ocherous steam off the stuff from the broken bottle.

He got a large suitcase, hurriedly dumped gadgets into it, then balanced the girl across his shoulder and carried both girl and suitcase down to his car, dumped them inside and drove off.

The girl was still acting as if she were asleep without actually sleeping. That is, she was limp, but her eyes were open.

Rush drove to the most convenient park and stopped in a lonely spot.

HE LOOKED at the girl. She had slumped limply on the seat, and she showed some of the signs of being intoxicated, but not all of them. She had limpid dark eyes, unusually perfect features, and a mouth which made Rush's toes want to curl a little.

"Who are you?" he asked.

He had to shake her before she answered. She seemed sleepy.

"My father was the murdered man," she said.

Rush frowned. The man Jonathan Noble was supposed to have murdered had been named Romero Enterline.

Rush thought he saw why she had been in his apartment.

"So you want the state to go ahead and electrocute Jonathan Noble?" he said. And added disapprovingly, "Whether he's guilty or not?"

The girl's voice had been low and thick. But now it was clearer.

"Young Noble is not guilty," she said.

"How do you know he's not?"

"I just know it."

"But why? You must have some reason."

"Because I love him," the girl said.

Rush frowned again. He had enough natural male instincts to feel irritated that another man should have the affections of a girl as pretty as this one.

"Are you engaged to him?" Rush demanded.

"Yes."

"But you're not married?"

"No."

"Always think twice before getting married," Rush warned. "Think several times." He rubbed his jaw while he got his mind back on the right track. "What were you doing in my apartment?"

"I was told to do what I could to help you."

Rush, astonished, asked, "Who told you to do that?"

"The voice on the telephone said to tell you it was Bufa. It said you would understand."

Rush scratched his head.

"I'm getting confused," he said. "Who were the men with whom we just had the big fight? Who was your father and why was he killed? Who is Jonathan Noble, and why was he framed?"

Instead of answering, the girl began to squirm around and rub her face.

"What have you done to me?" she asked.

Rush grinned. "You remember back in my apartment, when I shoved you in the closet?"

The girl nodded slowly.

"That is the last thing I recall," she said in a puzzled voice. "What is wrong with me?"

"That closet," Rush explained, "was rigged up as a gas chamber to administer a truth serum in vapor form which I've been experimenting with. The stuff seems to work. You've been telling a lot of truth."

"What kind of truth?" the girl asked anxiously.

RUSH WAS ordinarily a disciple of the truth. But like all detectives, he had learned that a little lying can work wonders if done in the right place at the right time. The end frequently justified the means, he believed.

He said untruthfully, "So you and the boy-friend put your heads together and murdered your old man, eh?"

"Boy-friend?"

"Jonathan Noble."

The girl looked completely horrified.

"If your truth serum made me say that," she gasped, "it does nothing but make a person tell awful lies."

"Then what would the truth be?"

The girl looked at Rush, obviously doing some thinking. At last, her lips curled in a way that was not complimentary to himself.

"I'm going to make up my mind about you," she said, "before I tell you anything."

Rush complained, "I don't understand that."

"I know you don't."

"Then why confuse me more? I'm plenty mixed as is."

She shook her head. "The whole matter is more important than you probably think. The welfare of a lot of people is vitally concerned."

"Now you're making me dizzy," Rush grumbled.

"I'll put it simply," the girl said.

"How simple?"

"My name is not Enterline, and my father's name was not Romero Enterline."

"That sure helps clear it up," Rush said disgustedly.

The girl continued, "If the newspapers got hold of my father's real name, and published the fact that he had been murdered, it would terrify a lot of people who think my father is going to help him. Those people would lose hope. As long as they think my father is alive, they will keep courage. As long as they have courage, they may go ahead and help themselves, we think. Now, isn't that simple?"

Rush started the car engine, drove out of the park and headed for a part of the city given over to rooming houses of the kind where not too many questions were asked.

"I keep a hide-out apartment rented," he said, "under a fake name. I go there when I get headaches."

CHAPTER IV

ADVERTISEMENT
FOR TROUBLE

THE HIDE-OUT APARTMENT was dark, grubby, impoverished; and practically its sole assets were three routes by which the tenants could depart in a hurry—a front door, a back one, and also a trapdoor which gave access to a stretch of rooftops and assorted fire escapes. If the neighbors were at all interested, which was unlikely, they believed the place was occupied by Mr. Thomas Ducker, a traveling salesman who was on the road a great deal.

"First," Rush said, "we both take a bath."

"But I don't need a bath," the girl protested.

"That's what you think."

Rush went into the bathroom. From the suitcase he had brought along, he removed a cardboard box which was labeled:

ELIXAR
THE PERFECT BATH SWEETENER

Rush ran the bathtub half full of warm water, dumped in part of the box of "Elixar," and stirred until the stuff was dissolved.

"Now," he said, "you get in the tub and stay five minutes."

"I won't do it!"

"Want me to undress you and give you the bath?"

"You wouldn't dare!" the girl snapped, and glared.

"With a figure like you've got, it'd be a pleasure."

"Oh!"

She entered the bathroom, locked the door, and he heard her in the tub.

"Full five minutes," he warned.

Later, she came out grimacing and fooling with her hair.

"What did you put in that water?" she demanded.

"Elixar, the Perfect Bath Sweetener."

"I thought it was a dead polecat."

Rush then filled the tub again, added more Elixar, and took his own bath. He sat for an entire five minutes completely submerged except for his nose, which he frequently held.

"Phew!" he said often.

He toweled himself, dressed, and walked back into the other room with jaunty steps.

"Great stuff, the Elixar!" he said. "Peps you up."

The girl made a face.

Rush sat down at the telephone and repeated the number which was on the instrument, several times to memorize it, then picked up the receiver.

The girl asked, "What are you going to do?"

"Advertise."

"What?"

"Sure. Advertising sells merchandise and makes the world go around, I've heard."

He telephoned each of the leading newspapers, and inserted a classified which read:

IF THE WHITE-HAIRED MAN WILL CALL
NATIONAL 0-1131, WE MIGHT MAKE A
BUSINESS DEAL.

"Now we'll set back," Rush announced, "and see if advertising pays."

THE GIRL spoke as little as the law allowed during the rest of that day. But she was pretty enough that even her silent presence was exhilarating. Furthermore, she showed no inclination to leave; so Rush was satisfied.

Late in the evening, Rush went out, bought newspapers, brought them back, and showed her the advertisement he had inserted.

"It sounds crazy," she said.

"I've got a knack for that."

"For what?"

"Zanies. They were my downfall as an inventor. I can't seem to think up anything that isn't fantastic. They call me that crazy inventor."

The girl studied him. "You're an odd one."

Rush didn't care for her tone. He'd been trying to impress her favorably, and had changed into a new neatly pressed brown suit—and shirt, necktie, shoes and socks all of matching browns—so that he cut a rather natty figure, he believed, even if his presence was a little rank from Elixar.

But she wasn't approving of him.

He sighed and pointed at the newspaper headlines.

"Look," he said. "The governor of the state says they can send me to the penitentiary for twenty years."

"Can they?"

"I don't know. If this keeps up, it may be the insane asylum instead."

"What makes you talk like that?" the girl asked sharply.

"What do you think? Here I am trying to save a man I've never seen from the electric chair. Some other fellows have tried to kill me to stop my saving efforts. And the girlfriend of the condemned man is here with me, but won't tell a thing because it might get in the newspapers." He looked at the young woman to see if she appreciated his troubles. "Don't you feel sorry for me?"

She shook her head.

"No, I'm not sorry for you," she said. "I'm just wondering how you got mixed in this."

"Why," Rush said dryly, "a toad told me to do it."

The girl winced, as if that was too much for her, and settled back with a sigh of resignation. If she was confused now, Rush wondered what state her mind would be in if she didn't know any more about the whole thing than he knew.

They were sitting there, looking as though each one thought the other a trifle whacky, when a funny-looking wooden bird came out of a clock on the wall and said, "Cuckoo! Cuckoo!"

The girl stared at the clock.

"Why, this is the first time that thing has worked today!" she exclaimed.

"Cuckoo! Cuckoo!" said the wooden bird.

"O.K.," Rush told the bird. He went to the window and looked out. "Nice and dark."

"What has dark got to do with that clock?" the girl demanded.

Rush pretended not to hear her, and from his suitcase he took a large black bag and a flashlight.

"Goin' snipe huntin'," he told her.

He climbed the stairs to the trapdoor in the roof. This trapdoor was heavy, old and rusty, but it opened as silently as a mouse going through a feather bed. Rush flowed out on the roof, took up a position behind a chimney and waited.

The roof was flat. The sky was dark. The traffic in the near-by street made a steady but low noise. Sounds of home life in the slums—babies bawling, wives complaining, and husbands yelling out what they had told the boss right to his face—was louder.

When a man came creeping around the chimney, Rush first squirted white flashlight glare into the fellow's eyes, then knocked him down, hit him again to make him senseless, and searched him. He collected three guns. Finally he put the bag over the man's head, shoulders and arms, and tied it around the fellow's waist.

The girl stared in astonishment when Rush arrived with the prisoner.

THE MAN in the sack started kicking. Rush selected one of the fellow's guns and clubbed the sack until it stopped jerking around.

He took the sack off and showed the man to the girl, as well as looked at the fellow himself.

The man was one of the gang of South Americans who had raided Rush's apartment under the leadership of the white-haired fellow.

His skin looked red and inflamed.

"What's wrong with his skin?" the girl asked.

"Know him?" Rush asked.

The girl nodded.

"Once upon a time, he was eleventh assistant secretary to my father," she said.

"How many secretaries did your father have?" Rush asked, eying her wonderingly.

"Nineteen," the girl said. "Of course, some of them were really secretaries to members of my father's cabinet. But it meant more to them to be called secretaries to the president, so we let them call themselves that."

"Your father was the president?"

"Yes."

"Of what?"

"Of a South American country."

"Was Jonathan Noble another secretary?" Rush asked.

"No. He was the bodyguard my father hired after we came to the United States."

In a patient voice, Rush asked, "And why was your father in the United States?"

The girl made a weary gesture with her shoulders.

"Where else could we go after the revolution?" she asked. "We wanted to be close enough to organize a counter revolution, so Europe was too far away. The United States was the only place where we thought we would be safe from the agents of the new government."

"But you weren't?"

"Not as it turned out," she said miserably. "The agents found my father, murdered him, and put the blame on Jonathan Noble." She pointed at the man Rush had captured. "He is obviously one of the agents of the new government."

Rush rubbed his jaw wonderingly. "You know, it does make sense after all."

"Of course. It is very simple."

Rush said, "You didn't want your country to be sure its ex-president was dead, because being without a leader might discourage the counter revolutionists?"

The girl nodded grimly. "The new president is a tyrant and a dictator."

"Politicians," Rush said, "always claim the other man is a tyrant and a dictator."

The girl started to object to that, but caught her breath instead and pointed.

"The light in the bathroom just went out!" she exclaimed.

"I saw it," Rush said. "I've been waiting for it to happen."

RUSH TOOK his flashlight and another black bag, but this time he also got a leather sack about the size of one of the long wieners which Frenchmen like. This was full of buckshot.

"These jaws are hard on my fists," he explained.

He went to the rear door, which was locked. He listened to someone trying a skeleton key in the lock, and waited until the person drew the key out to see why it was not working; after which Rush squirted a small amount of tear gas through the keyhole with his mechanical pencil gadget.

He opened the door a moment later and knocked another man senseless.

He searched and sacked this one, too, then carried him in and showed him to the girl.

This one also had a skin which looked as if it were terribly sunburned.

The girl said, "He looks as if he had been scalded."

"Another secretary?" Rush asked.

"No," she said. "He was one of the presidential chauffeurs."

After the explanation, she looked at Rush wonderingly.

"How could you tell they were around?" she wanted to know.

"Burglar alarms," Rush explained. "One of them is hooked to the cuckoo clock, and another one is fixed up with a relay to the bathroom light. If the light is off, and comes on—or if it is on, and goes off—there is a prowler around."

But the girl was still puzzled.

"How did they find us?" she asked.

"They got the telephone number from the advertisement I put in the newspaper," Rush surmised. "All they had to do then was go through the telephone book and find what street number the telephone belonged to."

The girl paced back and forth nervously. "What do you intend to do, anyway?"

"Keep on with my collecting," Rush explained. "And later, I'll try out my new truth serum on them.

She was still not satisfied. "But that advertisement— I don't understand—"

The white-haired man's voice spoke up.

"He's a hard guy to understand!" the man said.

CHAPTER V

LEG TROUBLE

RUSH GAVE THE surprised jump that he had almost given that time when he was sitting on top of the telephone pole at midnight. He came down flat-footed, with his hands in the air. The white-haired man's tone had told him that he had better get his hands up.

"Huh-how—huh-how—" He was so astonished that he stuttered, so he gave it up.

"I came in," the white-haired man said dryly, "while you were at the back door. After you got the man on the roof, we figured out that you had a burglar alarm rigged up here."

Rush shuffled his feet around on the floor. The floor was old, and it seemed to sag somewhat when he stepped on it.

The rest of the white-haired man's assistants entered. They had all come down through the roof trapdoor.

Each man's skin was reddish and inflamed.

"You're sure a half-boiled-looking bunch," Rush said dryly.

The white-haired man showed his teeth unpleasantly.

"What was the stuff in that bottle you broke on the floor of your apartment?" he snarled. "The stuff that looked yellow."

"A chemical," Rush said promptly. "It burns you, and the burn keeps getting worse and worse, and maybe you die."

"Can it be cured?" the man demanded.

"Sure," Rush said. "Sure it can."

"Then cure us!"

The other men had been acting as if they had a bad case of the itch which they were not supposed to scratch. Now one of them gave up the effort, and began to claw his red skin madly, making mewing noises of pain.

"This fellow was in the yellow stuff!" the fellow croaked. He jabbed a hand at Rush. "Why didn't it burn him, too?"

Rush said, "I took a bath."

"Bath, hell!" the man snarled. "We took baths first thing!"

Rush grinned. He began to see that his position was not so bad, but he still had trouble getting the grin to stay on his face.

"Elixar," he said. "You didn't put Elixar in the bath water."

The girl made a startled sound.

"Oh!" she gasped. "So that's why you took a bath in that horrible-smelling stuff, and made me take one!"

Her remark was exactly what was needed to convince the men that there was a cure for what was wrong with them.

"Search the place for some of that Elixar!" the white-haired man snarled.

THE SEARCH was conducted with frenzied speed, and netted them nothing. They came back and surrounded Rush and the girl in an ominous circle. The two men whom Rush had captured got to their feet and scratched themselves.

"I said in the advertisement," Rush remarked, "that we might make a deal."

The white-haired man growled, "What do you mean?"

"You confess to killing your ex-president, and get Jonathan Noble out of the penitentiary," Rush explained, "and I'll cure you."

"You think we're crazy?"

"Of course," Rush said, "if you didn't kill the president, that complicates matters."

The white-haired man fished in one of his pockets and got out a penknife, which he opened.

"Now, I'm going to cut one of your eyes out," he said grimly. "And I'm going to make you look at it with the other eye until you decide to cure us of whatever is wrong with us."

"And then you're going to kill me and the girl?"

"Of course not!"

Rush said, "It'd be danged inconvenient if you were a liar."

The girl had started trembling. He took her by the arm, led her to the table; she leaned against the table, grasping it tightly, her fingers seeming to take strength from the solidness of the wood.

Rush started patting his own pockets slowly.

"I'm going to smoke a cigarette while I think this over," he explained.

He never smoked.

"None of that!" the white-headed man snapped. "We've had enough trouble with your gadgets!"

Rush stared at them indignantly.

"Now look here, I want a smoke and I'm not in the mood to argue all day about it." He scowled and looked as firm as he could about the thing. "If you're afraid, one of you give me a cigarette and a match!"

There was some scowling back and forth, and finally the men gave in. One of them produced a cigarette; another a match.

Rush was careful not to move fast enough to excite anyone as he put the cigarette between his lips and scratched the match on the table. He held the cigarette on his lips, tilted upward, applied the flame to the end, and drew in smoke.

He held the burning match out to one side with his right hand, took the cigarette away with his left hand and held it up to draw attention to it.

"You smoke a good brand," he said.

He dropped the lighted match on the old rug. The match was still burning when it fell on the rug. There was a sputtering—the rug caught fire.

Instantly, a *whoosh!* The rug burned as though it were gunpowder. In a fractional second, greenish flame was all over the floor, and the room was full of stifling gray smoke.

Rush grabbed the girl, yanked her up on the table. They rolled off the other side, hit on the burning rug with Rush carrying the girl.

He ran with the girl, gained a door and went through. The men were too occupied with the fire around their feet to do anything to stop him.

The girl stared questioningly at Rush.

"That rug was one of my gadgets," Rush explained. "It's practically the same as made out of guncotton."

The men in the other room began making an uproar.

"If there's not enough tear gas left in that pencil," Rush said, "we may be embarrassed."

THE TWO police detectives did not look much like doctors, in spite of the white smocks which they had donned, the shiny mirror things for looking into people's mouths which they wore on their foreheads, and the stethoscopes they carried in their hands. They came out of the hospital room and found Rush in the hall.

Rush said, "I'll bet you didn't put it over!"

Both detectives grinned.

"Sure we did," one said.

"Two of them didn't actually take part in the killing of the ex-president," the other detective explained. "They broke down, and will turn state's evidence. We got a confession."

"What about Jonathan Noble?" Rush asked.

"The governor is going to give him a full pardon," one detective replied.

"What's the governor going to do about me?" Rush asked anxiously.

"He says to throw you in jail. He's hot about you playing on his belief in the supernatural."

"Why, the blasted politician!" Rush said indignantly.

The detective grinned. "The thing for you to do is run when we're not looking."

Rush asked, "Are you looking now?"

"No."

The girl was very grateful, but Rush's appreciation of her gratitude took a slide after she said, "Jonathan and I are going to be married as soon as he is pardoned."

"After what I told you about watching out for marriage!" Rush grumbled.

When Rush opened the door of his apartment—his other apartment, where the first fight had taken place—he saw that the yellowish vapor was still present in the room. The stuff would not kill a man, but it would burn painfully if not neutralized at once by the Elixar, and Rush had no liking for the odorous Elixar. He ventilated the apartment before going in.

The other half of the ten-thousand-dollar bill was under Bufa, the toad.

There was also a note.

"Glory be!" Rush chortled.

He was suddenly delighted. The owner of the voice of Bufa, the toad, had been here to leave half a bank note. The fellow had gotten into the yellow vapor. He would be burned. He would have to come to Rush for treatment.

Rush said cheerfully, "I'm finally gonna learn who that guy is!"

Then he read the note.

THAT ELIXAR SURE SMELLS, DOESN'T IT?
BUFA.

He dashed to the hiding place where he kept a supply of the Elixar.

Four boxes were missing.

Rush sat down, held his head with both hands, talked to himself violently, and wondered who in the name of mystery the voice of Bufa could be.

After a while, his head ached.

THE DEVILS SMELLED NICE

—BUT THEIR RACKET SMELLED
TO HIGH HEAVEN!

CHAPTER I

BIRD NEST SOUP

THERE WAS JUST one suspicious thing about the bird nest, but even that was not very noticeable.

There was never any bird around the nest.

Otherwise, it was a bird nest that looked ordinary, one that might have been constructed by any ambitious robin for the purpose of raising a family of chicks or whatever baby robins are called. It certainly looked like a common bird nest.

A great oak tree stood in the yard, a real giant of its kind, such a tree as the one under which the village smithy must have stood; and on a bough of this the bird nest sat. The oak had a profusion of leaves, and the leafage almost concealed the nest.

The leaves also hid a thin wire which ran out of the nest and along branches, and thence to another tree and finally into the window of a near-by apartment house. This wire was gray; from the ground it could have been mistaken for a spider web.

In the room in the apartment house, the wire was connected to a complicated electrical gadget which talked. The gadget was equipped with a loud-speaker which did not speak too loud; at least, not loud enough to interest the neighbors.

The bird nest was a pick-up antenna, being lined with innumerable turns of fine wire that had the advantage, even when seen at a short distance, of appearing to be the hair with which birds lined nests.

The whole arrangement was a device to eavesdrop on a telephone line. The telephone line ran from a house to a pole, passing within a few inches of the nest which sat so innocently on the oak bough.

So anything that was said over the telephone line reached the ears of Clickell Rush, who had been sitting— with what was for him unusual patience—in front of the pick-up amplifier.

Clickell Rush listened to the pickup for sixteen days.

He knew it was only a question of time.

In order that his hours would not be entirely wasted, he installed a temporary workbench in the apartment room and did some inventing.

In the sixteen days, he made two inventions. He invented a chemical paste which, if a little was smeared on a man, would make a whole zoo full of monkeys chatter in delight if the man came near. The stuff appealed to monkeys the way catnip fascinates cats.

Rush's other invention was a commonplace-appearing cigarette, the smoke from which would sting a man's mouth terribly—but only stung providing another chemical vapor was released in the air of the room at the instant the cigarette was being smoked.

Rush considered these two inventions typical of himself. So he was disappointed. He was disgusted.

He had a knack of inventing only things that were fantastic. He couldn't help it. He was like a farmer who had learned to raise peanuts, and everything he planted came up as peanuts. His mind worked that way, or something. Everything he invented turned out whacky.

He could reel off zany inventions the way a card shark deals bridge hands. But, so far, he hadn't been able to invent anything he could sell.

There had been a day when he hoped to peddle the inventions to police departments to use to catch crooks, but that day was gone. Police departments thought he was a nut, and they told him so.

On the seventeenth day of Clickell Rush's dickering, the conversation he had been awaiting came over the telephone wire.

ONE SPEAKER on the telephone—he was the next-door neighbor, and the gadget was eavesdropping on his telephone—had a voice which sounded as if someone had taken a crosscut saw to a board. Clickell Rush did not care for the voice, but he suspected his taste was evidently bad, because a million radio listeners thought it was swell; at least, radio surveys said a million listeners tuned in each week to get the voice.

"Hello!" it rasped.

One could understand why that voice had frightened innumerable criminals in the past.

"Hello!" the voice roared. "I can't understand you!"

It was exactly the tone that should belong to an old-man rhinoceros who had been the most famous crookcatcher in police annals.

"Speak up, dammit! Hello? Hello? What the hell is the matter with this connection?"

Clickell Rush grinned at his eavesdropping. He could visualize old Commissioner Cain, a beetle-browed and red-necked Beelzebub. Rush had never faced Commissioner Cain, but he'd seen plenty of newspaper pictures of the old crook-frightener.

"Is this Bufa?" shouted Commissioner Cain. "I'm calling somebody named Bufa! Hello! Hello?"

"*Yes,*" said a kind of replying strangle over the telephone. "*This is Bufa.*"

"Why the blasted blazes not talk so you can be understood? You got marbles in your mouth?"

"*Yes.*"

"What?"

"*I have marbles in my mouth,*" Bufa explained.

Commissioner Cain cut loose swearing. The old cop was noted for his profanity—in the radio studio, an engineer always had to sit at the control panels in tense readiness to cut extemporaneous cuss words from the salty program called, "The Cop Always Wins," which Commissioner Cain conducted Friday nights. This was the program that always started off with a loud knocking on a door and followed by the words: "Commissioner Cain! Open the door!"

"Will you explain why in damn-blast-it you've got marbles in your mouth?" Commissioner Cain yelled.

The difficult-to-understand voice of Bufa said, *"Now listen, Commissioner Cain—we might as well understand each other. You are a famous police officer, who has retired to conduct a popular radio program. No doubt you get a great deal of fan mail, and in this there must be occasional letters which tip you off to fantastic crimes. Am I right?"*

"Of course you're right."

Bufa continued, *"Six weeks ago, I wrote you a letter. The letter contained a telephone number, a thousand dollars, and a request. The telephone number was my own, the thousand so you wouldn't throw the letter away, and the request was for you to inform me of any fantastic crime that came to your attention."*

"What," growled Commissioner Cain, "d'you want with a fantastic crime?"

"Sh-h-h! It's a secret."

"You're a nut! A nut who had a thousand dollars."

Bufa chuckled. *"Matter of opinion, commissioner. Have you got a fantastic crime today?"*

"Whatcha think I'm callin' for?"

"Good," Bufa said. *"Come up to No. 90 Farview Drive, and tell me about it."*

"You'll be there?"

"I'll be there," Bufa said.

"O.K.," growled Commissioner Cain. "A thousand dollars is a thousand dollars, even from a crazy man."

AT THIS point, Clickell Rush yelled, "Boy, oh, boy!"

He grinned from ear to ear. He did a Queen o' the May around the eavesdropping gadget. He turned two handsprings.

"The day finally came!" he chortled.

He turned another handspring. He was a young man of average size who was equipped with muscles that seemed to be made out of the same material as fiddle strings, although otherwise he did not look outstanding. There were men more handsome than "Click" Rush to be seen on any street. He did have one eccentricity—Rush invariably wore clothes that were shades of brown. He was also known as the "Gadget Man."

He shook hands with himself.

"Fool me for months, will he!" he said gleefully.

He meant "Bufa." For months he had been trying to learn the identity of this Bufa, a strange individual who had thus far been only a voice.

Rush hurriedly put on a brown raincoat that almost exactly matched his brown suit. Clouds had packed the sky making the early evening unusually dark, and indicating that it might rain. He left the apartment, which he had rented under the name of Oliver Beaver, and galloped to his car, an inconspicuous-appearing coupé.

He looked and saw that there was a light in the neighboring house, in the room which Commissioner Cain used as an office; so, obviously, the old crime bloodhound had not yet departed for No. 90 Farview Drive.

"I can beat him to the place, all right!" Rush decided enthusiastically.

Rush only talked to himself when he was fit to explode with pleasure. He drove down the street.

This affair wasn't very sensible, he had to admit. But nothing in which Bufa was involved was ever quite rational.

Months ago. Rush had arrived in the big city with several trunks full of whacky inventions which he hoped to sell to the police department, which at once laughed at him. The newspapers had chuckled in print, called him the Gadget Man. Rush resented being called the Gadget Man. But what Rush resented most was Bufa. The best way of summarizing Bufa was to consider him—or her,

Rush didn't know which—as a ghost bull which Rush had once taken by the horns, and which had been chasing the Gadget Man ever since.

It had started when Rush came back to his room one day and found a small wired-wireless "transceiver" mounted in an imitation toad, and one half of a ten-thousand-dollar bill. There'd been instructions to hook the toad up to the city lighting system. Rush did so, and the toad began talking to him.

The voice speaking through the toad, Bufa, was a person talking over another "transceiver" somewhere in the city; so there was no way of tracing or identifying the person.

The thing was ridiculous right there; but it got worse.

Bufa wanted Clickell Rush to solve a fantastic crime, using the gadgets. Rush did so, and received the other half of the ten-thousand-dollar bill. He had been rather proud of himself.

But in the ensuing months, his pride got stuck full of thorns. Bufa had other unusual crimes to solve. A whole series. Bufa, it seemed, was a wealthy eccentric with a phobia for spotting unusual crimes and seeing them solved. Rush was supposed to do the solving. After he had been shot at a few times, he objected.

But refusing to work for Bufa did no good, for Bufa only dumped crimes into Rush's lap. Bufa perpetrated frame-ups. Rush found himself frantically solving crimes to clear himself. Bufa had outslicked the Gadget Man.

"Yeah!" Rush chortled. "But now I got him located!"

FARVIEW DRIVE must have been named by a humorist, because there was no far view anywhere on it, nor any view to speak of. It was a street in a suburb that had gone to seed, where there had not been a new house constructed for probably twenty years, and where in some places the houses that did stand had five and six empty weed-grown lots on each side.

Rush turned into the street.

"Boy!" he chuckled. "Am I going to get rid of an employer!"

He could think of an assortment of things he would maybe do to Bufa, none of them mild. For months he'd been trying to catch Bufa and convince him that he, Rush, didn't want to be a detective. His efforts had been remarkable failures. But now—success!

Rush knew Bufa located fantastic crimes by hiring well-known private detectives to report them. There was no more famed sleuth at the moment than Commissioner Cain. It was logical that Bufa would try to buy a fantastic crime from the grizzled commissioner. So Rush had tapped Commissioner Cain's phone line and listened patiently until he had proved his guess correct.

"That gets it in a nutshell," Rush grunted, having given the situation a mental review. "And *nut* is right!"

He drove past No. 90 Farview Drive and turned into a side street a block beyond, where he parked and switched off the lights. Due to the darkness, he had only been able to observe that No. 90 was a house, and there were vacant lots for blocks and blocks in each direction.

There was a low board fence around the house. Rush climbed this without trouble.

He crossed a shaggy lawn, wondering how he would explain himself to a policeman if one showed up. He could tell the cop he was sneaking up on the voice of a toad named Bufa.

"Hah!" Rush said.

The story would doubtless keep him out of jail, and just as doubtless land him in the place where they put feeble minds.

He decided to burst right into the house, grab Bufa, and start bouncing him off the walls.

The door was not locked. Rush shoved it open, stepped through. He was in a hallway faintly reddened by light from another room.

Sure enough, a man stood in the hallway.

"Bufa?" Rush asked.

"Hey!" the man said. "You're not—"

Rush said, "This is bird-nest soup!" and hit the man in the midriff.

Then another man, whom Rush unfortunately had not seen, stepped from behind the door, locked arms around Rush's neck, lifted Rush off the floor. The first man dived and grabbed Rush's threshing feet.

"Bounce him!" he gritted.

They slammed Rush on the floor, and Rush saw stars. The men fell on him, held him helpless.

"What'd he say when he came in?" one asked.

"Said it was a pleasure," the other stated.

CHAPTER II

THE THICKENING SOUP

THE EVENTS FOLLOWING Rush's ambitiously violent entrance had one thing in common with lightning striking—they had not taken long to happen. Two more men came running from other parts of the house, turned on the hallway lights and stared.

"Take a look outside!" ordered one of Rush's captors.

The two newcomers dashed outdoors and were gone for several minutes, then came back looking relieved.

"Car in a side street. Must be his. Nobody else around."

"Police car?"

"No."

Having examined the men, Rush was puzzled. They did not look like chauffeurs, butlers, bodyguards or other flunkies employed by the mysterious Bufa. They resembled businessmen more than anything else; prosperous, middle-aged, law-abiding members of the local Kiwanis Club—their faces had that brightly intent, we're-going-after-the-business expression. And there was one other thing they had in common—perfume.

Each man used perfume, and on each it was a different aroma. Four separate perfumes on the four men. Rush did not know much about perfumes, but this stuff smelled expensive.

Rush said, "Where is Bufa?"

They eyed him blankly, as if he had spoken a foreign language.

"He gets me," one of them said.

"He gets me, too," another admitted. "If it was back in Daniel Boone's day, you'd expect the Indians to come around."

"Where is Bufa?" Rush repeated.

They shook their heads blankly.

One man said, "Now I wonder what he means?" He came over and kicked Rush in the side. "What do you mean? Who is Bufa?"

Rush glared at him. "You don't know?"

"No."

"That makes us even," Rush muttered. "I don't know, either."

By now Rush had gotten the unpleasant impression that the men did not know anything about Bufa, also that they were in a deadly mood. There was no wild excitement in their speech, but there was something razor-edged about their manner.

Once Rush had visited a mine disaster and seen miners walk around with the same thing on their faces as these men—tension. That was it—tension in the presence of death.

"I wonder," Rush said, "what I've gotten into."

No one enlightened him.

There was a knock at the door. A hard, brusque knock. If a knock could have character, this one certainly had it.

"I'd almost bet my favorite radio program was starting," one of the men muttered. He took a gun out of a pocket, and the others also produced revolvers. The weapons were neat, inconspicuous and of good grade.

The first man leaned close to the door and asked casually, "Who is it?"

AT THE TOP OF THE STEPS,
HE MET THE DANGEROUS
END OF A GUN...

"Commissioner Cain! Open the door!" rasped a voice outside.

The man who was a radio fan breathed, "What the hell *am* I, a clairvoyant?"

THEIR ASTONISHMENT gave Rush a hollow stomach. They didn't know anything about the coming of Commissioner Cain. Nor about Bufa. And they seemed as calm as devils, and as bad.

It didn't make sense.

"Just a minute, until I get my clothes on," the radio fan said to the door. "You caught me taking a bath."

Then the man turned around, put the muzzle of his gun in Rush's left eye, cocked the weapon, and whispered, "Make a bleat and you'll have a bad case of brain scatter."

For moments indecision was a lighted bomb in the room; there was hot fear and blazing uncertainty, and the only cold thing was the snout of the pistol rooting Rush's eyeball.

"Something has busted!" a man hissed. "Busted wide open. We're not covered up any more."

The one with the gun said to Rush, "Walk backward, you!"

Rush backed down the hallway into a kitchen, the men bunched close to him, keeping him in danger from their guns. They turned out lights behind them. They glared at Rush.

"This guy—what about him?"

"He's seen us all."

"I know. That's what I was thinking."

One man fumbled in his coat pocket, took out a small wooden pillbox, which he uncapped. The pillbox contained a small glass bottle, which he dumped into his palm. Holding up the bottle, he said, "that law may stand outside for as long as five minutes. Do you think we've got time?"

"It won't take five minutes," another man said grimly.

The man with the bottle advanced on Rush. He showed Rush the bottle.

"Drink this," he ordered.

"What's in it?" Rush wanted to know.

"A harmless sleeping potion," the man explained. "It'll make you sleep for about three hours, and we need that long to get out of this mess."

"What mess?"

The man said, "Oh, hell! Drink it, or we'll make you!" He uncorked the bottle.

Rush got a whiff. He began to feel like the time he looked over the edge of the Empire State Building.

"That's hydrocyanic acid!" he said hoarsely. "It'll kill me instantly."

"Any time inside of five minutes will suit us."

All four men now laid hold of Rush and began trying to make him drink the poison.

Rush stepped on his left heel with the right foot and tore the heel off, then trampled on the small glass container of liquefied tear gas which the heel contained. He had not wanted to use the gas because he would be just as blinded as the others. But this had gone beyond a case of doing only what he wanted to do.

THE TEAR gas arose and the men began batting their eyes. "Gas!" they gasped. The man holding the phial of hydrocyanic got excited and dropped it. The phial broke, the acid sloshing over the floor and beginning to vaporize.

Rush knew that a whiff of the stuff could be as fatal as a drink, and a drink would kill a man almost before he got it swallowed.

Rush jerked free. He jumped clear of the group, crouched, leaped, grabbed the ceiling light chandelier. He did not expect the thing to hold him, and it didn't. It tore loose, and the room plunged into darkness.

The kitchen was furnished with a gas stove, and Rush felt for this. He found the stove, wrenched at it, tore it loose from its gas pipes, lifted it, hurled it at the men. The stove was heavy enough to floor an elephant. Judging from the sound, it did not hit anybody.

But gas began coming out of the broken pipes with the sound of someone whispering, "Sho-o-o-o-o!"

Rush felt for the kitchen cabinet and found something that felt like a salt shaker. He knew it is almost impossible to tell the source of a whisper in the darkness.

"Here he is!" he whispered.

Then he tossed the salt shaker. It hit a man. The man struck out. He must have swung great roundhouse blows calculated to floor anybody within reach, because he struck someone, and the latter must have clubbed a return blow with a gun. Down went the man who had been hit by the salt shaker.

Rush did not believe the man ever moved after he hit the floor. The blow must have rendered him senseless.

Vapor from the hydrocyanic on the floor began killing him.

The illuminating gas still made a *sho-o-o-o-o* sound. The pipe must be large, because gas odor was already strong in the kitchen.

Rush started to creep across the floor—and stepped into space. One moment there was a kitchen floor underfoot—then there wasn't.

Someone had opened a cellar trapdoor in the kitchen floor.

Rush cracked his head on something, slammed his shoulder on something else, and never did quite remember when he hit bottom. Upstairs, a man must have shot at the noise he made.

The gun flame set fire to the gas coming from the pipe. It was more of a gust of flame than a blast. Not enough gas had got out of the pipe to make a real explosion. There was a puff sound, red flame, very brief. Then men screaming.

The kitchen door banged. Men ran away. Two of them who were silent and one who was still yelling with pain from gas flame burns.

The blazing gas must have set fire to the wallpaper, for there was flickering red flame in the kitchen, and it sent dancing glows down the cellar steps.

Rush started to go up the cellar stairs. He was wondering what burning gas would do in the way of making hydrocyanic harmless.

Then a girl asked him a question.

"Why not cut me loose?" she suggested.

THEREAFTER, RUSH almost invariably thought of this girl whenever he saw a sunset. She was like that: dark and deliciously curved, and there was something about her that sparkled. Sparkled in spite of the ragged clothes she wore, and her fatigue, and her terror, for obviously she had been a prisoner here in the cellar for a long time.

"Ugh!" Rush muttered.

He meant her wrists, the way the handcuffs had chewed her. He'd never seen handcuffs like these before, the wristbands with sharp spikes which dug into flesh if the wearer tried to force them off, or wrench against them.

A chain fastened the girl's manacled wrists to a concrete pillar which supported the house over the basement.

Rush took one look at the solidness of the chain and did not even touch it.

"You wait here," he said. "I mean"—he added foolishly, remembering she couldn't move—"I'll find something to get you loose, and be back."

"If those four men are still around," the girl said by way of warning, "you may not be back."

Rush liked her courage.

But at the top of the steps, he met the dangerous end of a gun in the hands of Commissioner Cain. The gun was a large, old one.

"I'm bewildered," Commissioner Cain said, "and when I'm bewildered, I start shooting easy."

"We're both bewildered," Rush assured him.

Commissioner Cain had switched on the lights in the other rooms and their glow came into the kitchen. The commissioner stood, on legs stamped wide apart, like a crusty old gladiator who was accustomed to brimstone.

"You're under arrest," Commissioner Cain said.

Smoke swirled in the room and made it seem just the place for Commissioner Cain. The wallpaper had stopped burning. There were smoldering patches, however, on the clothing of the man who lay on the floor.

Commissioner Cain added, "Mind putting out the fire in the dead guy's clothes?"

Rush bent over the man who had been knocked to the floor during the fight. He held his breath, for he didn't know how strong the hydrocyanic might be. After he had held the wrist long enough to realize that the man was indeed dead, Rush let it drop suddenly.

"They'll probably electrocute you," Commissioner Cain said.

Rush stared at the old lawman. "You think I killed him?"

Commissioner Cain scowled.

"He's dead. You're here. You'll have to prove you didn't use that hydrocyanic on him."

RUSH WENT cold, then hot, trying to settle his feelings back to something approaching normalcy.

"I can prove I didn't," be said, "by the girl in the cellar."

"Girl? Cellar?"

"I'll show you."

They went down the cellar steps, and Commissioner Cain showed no noticeable surprise when he saw the girl; in fact, just after he saw the girl, Commissioner Cain began mumbling a demand as to whether the vapor of hydrocyanic acid was heavy and would therefore have settled in deadly quantities in the cellar, instead of blowing out of the kitchen when the door was opened, as he had been presuming.

Rush said, "This young woman will tell you how inno-cent I am."

The girl stared at them. Then she peeled her eyes until almost all the whites showed. "Yah, yah!" she said.

"Well, tell us about it," Commissioner Cain ordered.

"Yah, yah," the girl said. "I'm a little puppy dog on a chain."

"Why," Commissioner Cain said pityingly, "she's as batty as a bedbug."

"A puppy dog!" the girl said. *"Arf! Arf! Bow wow!"*

"You've driven her crazy!" Commissioner Cain snarled at Rush. "They'll electrocute you for this!"

CHAPTER III

THE RUNNING LADY

RUSH ROCKED BACK on his heels and felt as though astonishment had hit him like a club, and the impact had scattered his wits, dazed him, making him completely lose whatever grip he'd had on events that were flying around as senselessly as loose strings in a wind. He looked at the dark end of Commissioner Cain's old revolver; there, at least, was stable reality.

To the girl, Commissioner Cain said, "You poor kid! Where's the key to your handcuffs?"

"Arf!" the girl said. *"Arf! Arf!"*

"Hold your hands up," Commissioner Cain ordered Rush.

Forgetting that the cellar ceiling was low, Rush swung his arms up and skinned a knuckle on the joists, but he kept his arms up grimly, and Commissioner Cain approached and searched him thoroughly.

"What do you know?" Commissioner Cain grunted. "A bulletproof vest!"

Rush said to the girl, "You terrific liar!"

"Take that vest off!" ordered Commissioner Cain.

Rush removed the vest, making only necessary movements and doing those slowly, for he remembered that Commissioner Cain owned an impressive record for shooting crooks. The commissioner hefted the bulletproof vest, turning it over and over several times while he examined it, but never taking his gun menace off Rush.

"This is nice," he said. "Cops should wear something like this."

Rush had thought so, too, when he'd tried to sell the vest to the police department, it being one of his more sensible inventions.

Rush said, *"Arf! Arf!* I'm a big puppy dog!"

"What the hell!" Commissioner Cain growled.

"I just wanted to see if I could fool you, too."

"Find the key and turn that girl loose!"

Rush objected strenuously to searching the dead man upstairs for a key to the girl's handcuffs, for he had, above nearly all other things, a horror of corpses. But Commissioner Cain argued effectively with his gun, so Rush searched and found a key which fitted the cuffs. They turned the girl loose.

"Oh, thank you!" she said huskily.

"Poor kid!" Commissioner Cain growled. "Already she feels better."

He let her go ahead of them up the stairs, while he kept a close guard on Rush. When they reached the kitchen, he got a surprise.

Someone had lost a revolver on the floor during the fight in the kitchen, and the girl had picked this up. She had broken it open in her hands, and was examining to see if there were cartridges in the cylinder.

She pointed the gun at them.

"It's loaded," she said, quite sanely.

COMMISSIONER CAIN was flabbergasted. Had one of the microphones on his Friday night radio hour turned into a fist and clutched him by the ear, it would have been an event fully as unexpected as this.

"Wuh!" he said. *"Uh—wuh—"*

The girl got Commissioner Cain's old revolver. Rush could see that she was scared. She backed away from them quickly.

"Everything I've worked for all my life is at stake in this," she said, a tense desperation galloping with her words. "I'm desperate, or maybe I wouldn't do what I'm doing. I can't have you interfering."

She opened a door which admitted into a pantry used to store groceries. The place had no windows.

"Get in!" she said.

Rush began glaring at the girl.

"If you know what's good for you, you won't steal my car!" he said angrily. "It's in the street south of the house. You keep away from it! Hear me!"

The girl looked at him strangely.

"Get in the pantry!" she said.

It was dark in the pantry after she locked them in. Standing very still and listening, they heard feet leave the house, going swiftly with a rabbit patter. Then Commissioner Cain turned his beefy self around and knocked a can of beans off a shelf. The beans came down in a buckshot shower.

"*Arf! Arf!*" Rush said.

Commissioner Cain tried to slug him. Unsuccessfully.

"Damn that Bufa, whoever he is!" Commissioner Cain gritted.

"If we play like Bufa is the door," Rush said, "we might accomplish something."

They hit the door. The panel was stout, but they were savage, and before long wood splintered and they were out.

Rush knew exactly what he wanted to do and did it. He dived across the floor, scooped up Commissioner Cain's gun from a window sill where the girl had left it lying, and pointed the weapon at its owner.

"You've probably got some idea what a bullet from this thing will do to a man," he said. "I'm like that girl. I'm desperate."

Commissioner Cain's eyebrows got together on his forehead, like mice hugging each other for warmth. He pushed out his lower lip until it was almost a shelf.

They both heard, plain in the night stillness, a car motor starting, gears clashing, and the car leaving, bumping over the rutted pavement of Farview Drive.

"You made a sap move when you told her about your car!" Commissioner Cain growled. "She's took it."

"Did you come in a car?" Rush asked.

"Sure."

"Let's use it, then."

RUSH GAVE Commissioner Cain's automobile a dubious inspection. The vehicle did not have carbide gaslights nor did it steer with a tiller, but it appeared to be about that vintage. Rush kicked a fender, and a flake of rust the size of his palm fell off.

"Will it run?" he asked.

Commissioner Cain said a word vulgar enough to show that the jalopy was one of his pet eccentricities.

"You better navigate it," Rush decided.

The car, when it got in motion, lived up to worst expectations.

"We'll go to my apartment," Rush said. He gave the address.

Rush hung to the seat. The speedometer at once registered sixty, which was as high as it would go, but Rush judged, from the way everything on the street passed them by, that their speed was all of fifteen miles an hour. It sounded and felt like sixty.

"I've got you figured out," Commissioner Cain shouted over the speed and fury.

"You figured the girl was crazy, too."

"You're Clickell Rush, that bird they call the Gadget Man. I read about you in the newspapers, and one time I saw your picture. I only now placed you."

"You sound," Rush said, "unexpectedly friendly."

Commissioner Cain gave a snort that was famous over the air waves.

"Hell, why not? I've always had a sneaking admiration for you."

He then looked sidewise at Rush, letting the old car charge ahead with the disregard for traffic which seems to characterize the driving of old men who have been cops.

"How about appearing on my radio program?" he demanded.

Rush said, "I think I smell a buildup."

"Well," the old cop said, "I'd appreciate it if you didn't tell anybody how that girl fooled me."

"So that's it."

They reached their destination, and Commissioner Cain gasped at his own near-by home in astonishment, but said nothing. They entered the apartment where Rush had done the eavesdropping. Commissioner Cain narrowed one eye at the amplifier device which had listened in on his telephone line through the medium of the bird nest; his sniff indicated he recognized the purpose of the contrivance. He fell to scratching his head.

Rush got a gadget out of a closet. It was contained in a cheap suitcase. He signified that this was what they had come for, that they could now depart.

He said, "If you've got any idea what this mess is all about, you'd better tell me, on account of it might save us a headache."

"I haven't the faintest notion," Commissioner Cain growled.

LATER, RUSH got in the back seat of Commissioner Cain's old car, opened the suitcase, plugged a loop aerial into a jack installed in the top of the case, then removed a telephone headset and turned some switches.

"Bright kids play with these things," he explained.

"It looks like a radio direction-finder."

"It is."

"What'll it find?"

"The little radio transmitter on my car, I hope."

Commissioner Cain rubbed his jaw and scratched his head over that.

"You mean you had a radio all planted in your car? And it's switched on and sending now?"

"Yes."

"That," Commissioner Cain said, "doesn't seem like something that a sensible man would do."

The reaction did not hurt Rush's feelings; he had encountered it before. He had come to accept the fact that persons just naturally considered him whacky when they heard about one of his gadgets.

He offered a slight explanation. "It's a theft hook-up for an ordinary car radio that I was trying out. If a secret switch isn't thrown, the car receiver becomes a low-power, shortwave transmitter putting out a continuous signal. If the car is stolen, it can be located with a directionfinder." Rush scowled darkly. "You know what the country's biggest maker of car radios did when I tried to sell him the gag? He laughed at me."

"I don't blame him," Commissioner Cain said. Then he gave the matter second thought and rubbed the end of his nose. "But there's something catchy about the idea, at that."

Their course took them toward the central part of the city, then past the theatrical district, which was brightly lighted and crowded, a fact that surprised Rush, for it had seemed to him that it should be later in the night.

Suddenly old Commissioner Cain banged his knee with a hand.

"It'd wow 'em!" he yelled.

"What would?"

"You could go on my radio program and tell about these things you've invented to catch crooks. The radio listeners would eat it up!"

"Still trying to bribe me not to mention the *Arf-Arf* girl to the newspapers, eh?"

"Well, what about it?"

"No!" Rush said. "Enough people think I'm crazy as is. Anyway, aren't you thinking about this thing we're trying to solve now?"

"What good would thinking about it do?" the old cop asked.

They left the theatrical district behind and entered a manufacturing section. Rush took more bearings. They continued driving, and finally passed Rush's car. They went on two blocks, and stopped.

Rush said, "The way I figure it, the men took something from the girl. Then they held her so she couldn't tell anybody about it."

"I think you might be right," Commissioner Cain agreed.

"After the girl left us, she went after the men," Rush added.

"And we're after everybody."

They left the car, scuttled in haste to shadows packed along the side of a windowless brick building that extended the length of the block.

The water front was very close; they could smell salt water and hear the night harbor sounds.

Rush's car stood before a three-story structure of brick that was a little neater than the other buildings around about. There was a door which glowed faintly red, as if a night light burned somewhere inside.

The first glance inside showed the man sprawled on the floor. A middle-aged man in overalls.

"The night watchman!" Commissioner Cain muttered.

A time clock that lay beside the prone man made his occupation evident.

Rush bent over the man.

"He's alive."

"I'm gonna telephone for cops," growled Commissioner Cain. "After all, I have retired from police business."

He started outdoors.

The watchman came to life, turned over and showed them the pistol on which he had been lying.

"We can't have any cops here!" he growled.

CHAPTER IV
PERFUME BUSINESS

THE WATCHMAN WAS small, wrinkled, chinless; he was a totally unimpressive figure in the worn overalls. His hands were thin, and the veins on their backs were black enough to seem pulsing full of ink.

"Hey!" he yelled.

The shout brought two men from the back of the building. The pair had been at the Farview Drive house earlier in the night. At the house, they had looked well-dressed, immaculate, each carrying on his person the trace of a distinctive perfume; now they were stripped to undershirts, their hair was tousled, their hands and bare arms were dust-soiled, and if they smelled of anything, it was of the perspiration which streamed from them.

"Look," the watchman said. "These guys come in and start talk about callin' cops, and I don't know what to do."

The two men stared grimly.

"What you done was all right!" one said.

The speaker jumped over, wrenched the gun out of the watchman's hand, pointed it at Rush, and cocked the weapon.

"Wait!" barked his companion.

"What for?" snarled the man with the gun. "The boat's loaded, ain't it?"

"Yeah, but—hell's bells!—let's think a minute."

"Then we better take 'em on the boat."

The watchman whinnied, "You want me to stay here and go on pretendin' I've been slugged?"

One of the perspiring men went to the door and stood listening for a time. Something—either the night air or his own thoughts—made him shiver.

"Yeah," he told the watchman. "You go on pretending you've been slugged. If any cops come, revive and tell them it was robbers hit you, and they drove away in a truck. A *truck*, understand? While they look for a truck, we can skip in the boat."

"Sure."

Click Rush and Commissioner Cain were searched, then led into the back of the building, where there was another door. They passed through this out onto a dock built at the back of the brick structure.

To the dock was tied a boat. Rush, who was something of a boat bug, recognized it as a stock model cabin cruiser, about forty-six feet on the water line, a yachty craft which looked trim and racy, but probably could not do over twenty knots at top speed.

The third perfumed man was waiting tensely beside the cruiser with a gun in his hand.

He put a flashlight beam on Rush and Commissioner Cain.

"These are the same two who turned up at the house!"

"Sure."

"But the girl said she hadn't told anybody what was going on. She said she didn't know these guys, hadn't ever seen 'em before, and had no idea how they came to turn up at the house. She said she didn't tell them she was coming here."

"She lied to us."

"I guess she did."

The gun muzzles herded Rush and Commissioner Cain aboard the cruiser. In getting on the craft, they stepped first into the deckhouse, a glassed-in inclosure about twelve feet wide and a little longer, which was fitted with upholstered transom seats and contained the steering wheel, clutch lever, compass binnacle and so on.

At least a score of strong wooden packing cases were arranged on the deckhouse floor. All the cases seemed to be labeled:

ESSENCE ROBARD, GRASSE.

Rush eyed the boxes.

"Now I begin to get this," he muttered.

COMMISSIONER CAIN scowled at the boxes, then at Rush, for obviously he didn't get anything. Being puzzled seemed to aggravate him, and he blew out his cheeks indignantly.

One of the men said, "Get down below."

There was a small cabin forward, just off the deckhouse, the only exit being back through the deckhouse.

The girl was sprawled On the floor, tied hand and foot with rope.

Rush said, "You seem destined to spend your life in ropes or chains."

Commissioner Cain glared at her. "Insane, eh?" he snarled.

She did not say anything.

Rush and Commissioner Cain were forced to sit on the floor near the girl.

The perfumed man who seemed to be spokesman said, "There's a light anchor and a heavy one forward. Get them. Get some rope, too."

One of the others said, "The anchors may be traced."

"They're not numbered. We'll tie the girl and this guy in brown to the heavy anchor." He scowled at Commissioner Cain. "We'll give you an anchor all your own."

Commissioner Cain swallowed and eyed Rush. "They're gonna dump us in the harbor!"

Rush did not feel that an answer was necessary; anyway, he doubted that his voice was in any condition to manage one. He was scared. He often thought he could get seven times as scared as an ordinary man.

A man went to get the anchors.

It was quiet inside the cabin. Harbor noises seemed to have stopped, and there was no sound of waves against the hull. One of the perfumed men wiped perspiration off his forehead, using his hand which did not hold a gun.

Then Commissioner Cain deliberately gathered his legs under him and rested his knuckles on the floor.

"Damned if you're gonna kill me!" he said harshly. "Not without me doin' somethin' about it!"

He was, Rush saw, going to fling himself at the nearest man—and probably get himself shot.

Rush said, "Let's don't die ignorant."

The old cop turned his head. "Huh?"

"We might as well be sure what this is all about," Rush said. "Did you ever hear of Grasse?"

Commissioner Cain scowled. "Hello, no. It's on them boxes. 'Essence Robard, Grasse.' But it don't mean nothing to me."

Rush looked at the girl.

"Grasse," he said, "is the great perfume center in France. Perfume is expensive. For a dollar, you hardly get a thimbleful of the really good stuff."

"The devil with perfume!" Commissioner Cain snarled. *"They're gonna kill us!"*

"Perfume," Rush continued, "is often made out of essence which is diluted. Even after it is diluted, you still pay a dollar for a thimbleful of the perfume. So the essence must be pretty valuable."

One of the perfume men ordered, "Shut up!" But he was not violent about it—all of his tense attention was spent in watching desperate old Commissioner Cain.

Rush said, "Those packing cases in the deckhouse must be full of perfume essence." He looked at the girl again. "What are they worth?"

"Over a hundred thousand dollars," she said, tensely.

"These men stole them from you?"

She nodded. "From me and the perfume company in which I'm a junior partner."

Rush asked, "And why were they holding you?"

"To make it look like I stole the essence," the girl said stiffly. "They framed their thieving onto me."

Rush blinked. "And that's why, back at the house, you wouldn't tell us the truth? That's why you played crazy?"

"Of course. I'm an accused thief. You would have arrested me. And by the time I made you believe me, these men would have gotten the cases of essence out of the building here, where they had hidden them, and would have gotten away. I came to stop them myself." She bit her lips. "I didn't have such good luck. I didn't know the watchman was working with them. I asked him to help me. And he grabbed me."

The man returned with the anchor.

RUSH HAD torn the heel off his left shoe earlier in the night when he had released the tear gas. But there was still a heel on his right shoe. Now he put his left toe against this, as if he were going to tear that one off.

He pointed at the heel.

"How would you like another dose of gas?" he demanded loudly. "Poison gas, this time!"

The three perfumed men stared wildly at the heel. Their attention was distracted.

Then Commissioner Cain sprang. He hit the nearest man, floored him. The other two wheeled with their guns. Rush leaped and shouldered one into a bulkhead. The man Commissioner Cain had hit fell near the girl, and she flung herself, bound as she was, across him, holding him down, for the man was not entirely out.

There was only one man on his feet with a gun now.

Both Rush and Commissioner Cain charged that man, Rush holding the fellow he had trapped with his arms. They wedged against the gunman. The man jammed his weapon at Commissioner Cain and fired. The old cop barked and collapsed.

Rush clubbed a fist at the gunman's arm. The gun flew away. Rush, clutching furiously, managed to get a hold on both men, but one slugged him in the stomach, and sickness jumped all through him.

Madly, Rush lunged. He got going with both men, charged across the cabin. They hit a bulkhead, one man with his head, and that one went limp.

Rush went back across the small cabin with the remaining man and dived at another bulkhead. He always thought that his own head hit the wall fully as hard as did the skull of his victim, but the other man became senseless, and Rush didn't.

Rush got one of the guns and went around rapping skulls just to make sure the three were senseless.

"Was there anything in that heel?" Commissioner Cain barked.

"Just imagination," Rush admitted.

Commissioner Cain took hold of his right leg between hip and knee and fell to making awful grimaces.

"By damn!" he yelled. "The devils smelled nice, but they've shot my leg off!"

BY THE middle of the next afternoon, Commissioner Cain made enough recovery that, when Rush came into the hospital room, the old cop was yelling at a doctor how damned well he could walk if they would just tell him where they'd hidden his clothes; and the doctor was trying to explain that a bullet which had nicked a leg bone made a wound that was not to be trifled with in that fashion.

"Arf! Arf!" Rush said.

Commissioner Cain took the bird nest off the night table and handed it to Rush.

"I had a cop climb the tree and get this," he explained. "And you aren't kidding me. You didn't tell anybody about how that girl fooled me." He snorted. "Not that I would have cared if you had."

Rush took the bird nest.

He said, "The way the district attorney is talking, it'll be a wonder if they don't hang our three perfumed devils."

Commissioner Cain pointed at the bird nest. "I don't like the blasted idea of guys eavesdropping on my telephone line!"

"I'm still puzzled," Rush continued. "There was a newspaper story about the disappearance of the girl and the theft of the perfume essence. The story came out about a week ago, when it happened. Bufa reads the newspapers, and spots fantastic crimes that way; so probably that's the way Bufa got onto this one.

"How'd Bufa know they were keeping the girl in that house?"

"Probably shadowed the perfumed men and decided there was something phony about the way they ganged up at the house. The men were all employees of the girl's perfume company; hence they're probably logical suspects to Bufa."

"Humph!"

Rush set the bird nest on Commissioner Cain's head like a cap, and the grizzled old cop knocked it off.

Rush said, "Where is that fan letter you got? The one you called Bufa about."

Commissioner Cain selected a letter from a pile on the night table. "This one."

Rush read:

> *There is a girl and she may die unless someone looks for the perfumed men.*
>
> *And it is time that soup was made out of that bird nest, anyway.*

Rush hurled the letter on the floor. "Bufa sent this!" he yelled. "It's Bufa's handwriting!" He thought of all the time he had spent listening in on the phone line, thinking he was finally going to get a clue to the identity of Bufa. He kicked the letter. "Bufa knew I was eavesdropping with that bird nest all the time!" he gritted.

Commissioner Cain grinned derisively. "I got another letter this morning," he said. "There was an envelope inside addressed to you. Here."

Rush tore the envelope open and found a ten-thousand-dollar bill.

He started off very well with his exasperated swearing, but it was hard to keep it up with all that money in his hands. He wound up with a sheepish grin.

"When is that girl coming to see me?" demanded Commissioner Cain. "She's a looker."

"We'll be past later," Rush said—"on our way to a night club."

Commissioner Cain glared at him. "Take your bird nest and get out of here! I've had enough of Bufa!"

"I've had enough for some time," Rush said.

ABOUT THE AUTHOR

LESTER DENT (1904–1959) was a cock-eyed wonder. Born in La Plata, Missouri, he grew up on ranches and farms throughout Wyoming, Oklahoma and Nebraska, where he experienced the waning days of the pioneer West and devoured stacks of pulp magazines. He later claimed his lonely childhood fired an imagination that went on to create concepts and characters which still reverberate in popular culture a century later.

Early in life, he knocked about various professions, was a cowboy, a sheepherder, sold shirts, and worked in a broker-age house. He briefly studied law, and almost went into banking.

Settling down in Tulsa, Oklahoma, Dent became a tele-graph operator, working in the wire rooms and tiger cages of oil companies and newspapers. As a teletype mainte-nance man toiling for the Associated Press in the Tulsa World Building in 1928, he discovered a fellow worker writing a pulp story. When Dent learned what the pulps were paying, he decided that he was destined to be a writer. This abrupt decision was not entirely whimsical. Hs favor-ite author was *Black Mask's* Dashiell Hammett, and faith-fully every Wednesday, he read his favorite pulp, *Argosy*. Going back to ranching days, Lester used to sneak into the cowboy's bunkhouse to devour the stacks of pulp magazines stored there for entertainment and hygienic purposes.

Dent jumped into the field during the pulp magazines' romance with Charles A. Lindbergh, the lone aviator who soloed across the Atlantic in 1927. All America had become "air-minded," so Dent's earliest yarns starred barnstorming pilots. The economy was booming. There was big money in pulp fiction.

The stock market crash of October 1929 changed all that. Pulp markets began drying up. Dent had trouble selling. He refused to give up. Branching out, he wrote detective, air-war and Western stories. Magazines folded up as fast as he could submit to them. The Roaring 20s were truly over. It was a discouraging time.

Late in 1930, with the Great Depression coming on, Lester Dent was offered a position as staff fiction writer by Dell Publications in New York. It meant abandoning a highly-paid technical career akin to being a computer technician today. But Dent yearned to see far places and do different things.

He and his wife Norma landed in the big city the first week of January, 1931. For the next five months, Lester wrote novelettes and short stories for *Sky Riders* and *Scotland Yard*, as well as radio scripts for the *Scotland Yard* radio program.

Only two years in the fiction business, his editor described Dent as "...one of the grandest purveyors of ripping, tearing, he-man action-fiction who's loomed over the magazine horizon in many a long year..." And Lester was only getting started.

When Dell abruptly folded its Depression-battered pulp line that spring, Dent discovered that the entire fiction field had gone flat. Moving back to La Plata to live with his parents, the Dents regrouped. Lester was effectively jobless in the Great Depression. Yet he still refused to surrender his dream. Having tasted the writing life, he could not return to the ordinary working world.

Gradually, Lester broke into new markets. Readers and editors alike loved his exuberant yarns spun in an infectious style. By the new year, he was back in Manhattan, grinding out pulp in all genres, often making the covers of titles like *Detective-Dragnet* and *Western Trails*. His work attracted the attention of Street & Smith, to whom Dent had sold his first four stories.

The Shadow was mesmerizing America on radio and in the pages of a new kind of pulp magazine. The company that in dime-novel days had given the world Nick Carter, Frank Merriwell and Buffalo Bill was gearing up to launch a fresh generation of paper heroes. One was to be called Doc Savage. Street & Smith thought Lester Dent would be the perfect writer to bring their Supreme Adventurer to life. He had just turned 28.

After writing a test Shadow novel, Dent began chronicling the exploits of the Man of Bronze. It was December 1932, the end of the Depression's darkest year. Simultaneously, The Lone Ranger was being created. Conan the Barbarian had just been born. Max Brand's Silvertip was debuting of Street & Smith's *Western Story Magazine*. All three heroes would go on to great multi-media fame, but none would have the lasting cultural impact of Doc Savage.

It was the beginning of the greatest creative period in the young writer's life. Over 150 electrifying Doc Savage novels would emerge from Dent's Royal typewriter, along with two dozen Doc radio scripts. Yet almost all of them appeared under a house name Lester neither devised nor desired.

Although he would go on to crack all of the most prestigious pulp markets he aimed for—*Argosy, Adventure,* and *Black Mask*—as well as slick magazines like *Colliers'* and *The Saturday Evening Post,* the career of Lester Dent as Lester Dent was drawing to a premature close. He was now and forever "Kenneth Robeson"—immortal, yet not truly himself.

When he did surface as himself, he hit home runs. Two of the most-anthologized stories ever to come out of the pages of the legendary *Black Mask* magazine were bylined Lester Dent. Featuring Miami private eye and boat owner Oscar Sail, they read like blueprints for John D. MacDonald's Travis Magee series.

Beginning in 1932 with his Lynn Lash stories, Dent also pioneered the concept of the sleuth who used tricky scientific gadget solve crimes. Other included Jee Nace, aka the Blond Adder, and Foster Fade, the Crime Spectacularist. This specialization culminated in the Doc Savage series, as well as Dent's long-running *Crime Busters* series featuring inventor Click Rush, the Gadget Man. Dentian gadgetry was subsequently appropriated by latter-day superheroes.

After World War Two, Dent found time to write mystery novels. *Dead at the Take-Off* and its sequel, *Lady to Kill,* introduced Chance Malloy in 1946. *Lady Afraid* and *Lady So Silent* exploited Dent's days knocking about the Miami sailing community, and showcased his versatility by featuring strong female protagonists. *Smith is Dead* was a forerunner to the type of crime-suspense novels he would write for the emerging paperback book industry.

After a successful 16 year run, *Doc Savage* was cancelled, along with the rest of Street & Smith's pulp chain in 1949, freeing up Lester to write whatever he chose. But the death of his parents coupled with the loss of three fingertips suffered while cutting lumber in his basement put him in no frame of mind to do any more than dabble in the emerging paperback book market.

Yet out of this period came *Cry at Dusk, Lady in Peril* and *Honey in his Mouth,* which Hard Case Crime brought out in 2009 to rave reviews, cementing Dent's reputation as top suspense writer.

For three years, Dent ran Airviews, an aerial photography service he created. It peaked with a fleet of five planes, including Dent's personal ship.

Taking over the dairy farm which had been in the family for nearly 100 years, Dent brought scientific methods to the challenges of modern farming. He is credited with being the first to bring Grade A milk into his corner of Missouri, and after decades of traveling, appeared content to live the quiet life of a gentleman farmer. He passed away at the age of 54, in 1959, just as the last surviving pulp magazines were going out of business, victims of television, the paperback revolution, and changing times.

Lester Dent died thinking his name and works belonged to a pulp past destined to be forgotten. Just a year before his passing, he scoffed at the mention of his old Doc Savage novels, saying, "They would be so outdated today that they would undoubtedly be funny. Hell, when I wrote them, an airplane that could fly 200 miles per hour was science fiction. They would be of no interest any more."

Five years after his death, Bantam Books released three Doc novels to test a market in which pulp reprints of Edgar Rice Burroughs' Tarzan of the Apes were selling briskly. Thanks in part to James Bama's powerful monochromatic covers, Doc Savage sales surged and surged until millions of copies were sold, making "Kenneth Robeson" one of the best-selling authors of the 1960s—a posthumous vindication which, for all his imaginative powers, Lester Dent himself never envisioned.

Dent has been called the Father of the Modern Superhero, and with good reason. As the co-creator the perennially popular Doc Savage, he laid the foundation for generations of superheroes to come. Superman owes much of his mythos, as well as his Fortress of Solitude, to the Man of Bronze. Batman borrowed his scientific training and utility belt filled with ingenious gadgets. The format of the Doc Savage series was a major inspiration for Stan Lee and Jack Kirby's ground-breaking Fantastic Four, which spawned the Marvel Universe. The creators of landmark series ranging from The Man from U.N.C.L.E. to The Destroyer have acknowledged the Doc Savage influence.

One can trace the roots of heroes as diverse as *Star Trek's* Mr. Spock and *The X-Men's* Beast back to the pages of *Doc Savage Magazine*. And James Bond's world-famous cinematic gadgets owe more to the inventive genius of "Kenneth Robeson" than they do to Ian Fleming. And what are Clive Cussler's Dirt Pitt and Buckaroo Banzai but updatings of the Man of Bronze?

Sixty years after he left us, Lester Dent's works remain in print, lost stories continue to trickle out, and his rich legacy continues to grow.